I0673095

HELLO BERLIN!

JASON S. ANDREWS

TRUTH SERUM PRESS

TRUTH SERUM PRESS

ISBN: 978-1-925536-11-9

Truth Serum Press
4 Warburton Street
Magill SA 5072
Australia

Email: truthserumpress@live.com.au
Website: http://truthserumpress.net
Truth Serum Press catalogue: http://truthserumpress.net/catalogue/

Front cover image by Jason S. Andrews
Back cover image and jacket design by Matt Potter
Author photograph by Amy Withey

Also available as an eBook
ISBN: 978-1-925536-12-6

for

Caitlin

5th March 2005

'Ost' is German for 'east'. 'Nostalgie' is German for 'Nostalgia'. 'Ostalgie' is the yearning for old East German kitsch like the Ampelman (the GDR traffic light man who wears a hat and is branded on many tourist-friendly merchandises) and I'm surrounded by it in Ostzone, a darkly rouge-lit bar hidden under the rail tracks in Mitte.

It's probably my fifth beer. Fifth beer translates to drunk, as Berlin-beer's sold cheaply by the half litre. Saves trips to the bar but the last third is always tepid. Posters of Erich Honecker, Karl Marx and Dynamo Dresden Football Club are spinning.

There are a few locals about, surely not too happy about a group of twenty tourists stomping through here on a pub crawl. I stumble to the bar and sense someone's stare; a woman with soft, brown hair and a slim figure, I don't realise the full extent of her age until she's standing beside me.

She stares unbreakingly, confident, knowing; and talks so close to my face I'm practically pinned against the wall behind me. But her voice is something, low and smooth. We exchange words. She asks if I recognise her. I don't. She doesn't believe me. I shrug.

She tells me she sings in a band and does some acting on television, as if that will help me realise who she is.

'I'm English,' I say as way of explanation, which must be obvious as we're speaking English. The only German bands I've heard of are Kraftwerk and Rammstein.

'Are you sure you don't recognise me?'

The bushy bearded barman raises his eyebrows at us. She's there and it's cheap, so I buy her a drink. I figure that's why she timed her approach, but she won't let me go. She tells me where she's from, when she started singing, her favourite music, how great the nearby Strandbar is...

I don't know if we agree to leave together or if I need the fresh air to stop the spinning and she follows me, but the next thing I know, we're walking along the river together and she's singing in my face to show me what a great voice she has. I've left my friends without saying anything, which they were disconcertingly nonchalant about.

We walk a few yards east to the Strandbar – all palm trees and ambience, imported sand and deck chairs. Green light illuminates the austere stone of the Bode Museum opposite, hovering over the Spree glistening calmly in the moonlight. A Taj Mahal steel drum album plays and she talks about herself with her unbreaking stare. I look back at her with a fixed, relaxed-looking smile though I'm wondering if it's just loneliness that's wrong with her, how I can get away from her and – if I do – work out where the hell I am.

Then she says she wants to see her friends in Silberfisch and off we go. This bar is one of the only places on Oranienburger Strasse not to have been replaced by big Thai, Italian or Indian restaurant/bars on what's become the big tourist strip and red light district. Women of the night stand around in spandex outer-space outfits; you feel guilty for ignoring them, but offer eye-contact and they don't leave you alone. Overlooking it all is the golden crown of the Neue Synagoge, the sole reminder that this was the old Jewish quarter; the only synagogue to survive the pogroms because the local police officer on duty that night declared the building was a protected historical landmark and demanded the Nazi mob disperse.

Her friends in Silberfisch consist of friendly bar staff who pour us free drinks. 'This is the greatest barman in Berlin,' she says of the handsome, dark-haired boy behind the bar. 'He'll use the best quality alcohol and makes drinks with the perfect measurements. You'll get a hangover but you won't be sick.'

'Great.'

People are noticing her. Strangers approach just to say a sheepish hello. I'm handed free drink after free drink. We drink the bar dry. We dance on the small dance floor at the back. She keeps on talking at me and I continue my efforts to look interested.

We get a Döner (kebab) at the bottom of Rosenthaler Strasse and fall against the bar in 'Delicious Donuts' opposite. My hangover is setting in and I'm disappointed they don't actually sell donuts; we're there for morning Bloody Marys. I'm still wondering how to politely part from her but the right moment never comes. She never pauses. It's like being with a beautiful woman waiting for the right kiss-her moment, except that I'm waiting for the right moment to make a polite getaway.

I want to be alone, to collapse in a dark room to groan and flatulate, but she charms two men into lending us their bikes and we ride to her place in Schöneberg on the west side of town as dawn breaks.

I'm too spaced out to pay much attention to the building. It's some kind of commune, the large hallway filled with dozens of bikes leaning against each other like a junkyard. At the end of the hall is a grand set of baroque double doors that open onto a large courtyard. We walk up some stairs, collapse on a bed and hold onto each other for dear life for the entire morning.

6th March 2005

We doze for the first half of the day. My friends text about our impending flight home. My brain and fingers manage to collaborate a brief reply saying I'm fine but I won't be coming. As for my job, it's one of those hangovers where you're so focused on staying alive, missing a plane or losing a job is small stuff.

Eventually the pain subsides enough so I'm able to drink some water handed to me. I take in my surroundings. It's all so large, the windows, the bed, the space around me. 'What is this place?' I ask.

'The Bowles,' she answers proudly, a gorgeous *Alt-Bau* (high-ceilinged, pre-war courtyard-building) and for twenty-five years, a famous West Berlin squat so-named for its location on Bowles Strasse.

Her skin is as soft as her speaking voice and a floral tattoo accentuates the delicate contours of her neck and back. She is slow in her moves and trembles to the touch as she presses herself against me.

'I have to ask you something,' I say in all seriousness.

'What?' her smile suddenly a look of concern.

'What's your name?' I ask, not without embarrassment.

'If you don't know now, I'm not telling you.'

'Ok.'

'I think it's sexier that way.'
'Sure.'
'More mysterious.'
'Ok.'
Her mysteriousness lasts five seconds. 'It's Anja.'
'Oh right.'
'Are you sure you've never heard of me?'

11th March 2005

We spend most of our time in bed, but manage to get outside for a couple of walks. Berlin still has the sense of a frontier town; walking along a commercial high street, you can turn a corner and empty landscape confronts you. The city was so annihilated in the Second World War, and was then split into two cities during the Cold War. The east side suffered from the backward ways of the GDR regime, so the empty-spaces / missing-buildings / empty-buildings situation didn't change much. West Berlin became an isolated island stuck in the middle of the GDR, so it too had its problems. After the Berlin Wall fell, suddenly there was all this space and all these empty buildings, many of which acquired unofficial residents who stayed for so long that contracts transpired and all became official.

The Berlin squats – especially the newer, less official ones in the east – are being phased out as Berlin builds itself up to be Europe's trendiest city and an economic power, and soon won't exist anymore. But the Bowles should be alright as it's been around for so long. Time will tell.

Around thirty people live here but it's not at full capacity, they share a dozen or so communal kitchens and luxurious manicured garden terraces; they lock the front door and the rest is open house.

It's not as punk as the other squats (therefore I guess clever enough to still exist). Some of the residents have lived here for over twenty years, have grown up, lost their leather and cut their hair. Some still have an over-dependence on weed and alcohol. The real museum piece here is Raybay, an ageless dread-haired pierced-faced spike-and-chain-wearing die-hard punk who only ever goes out for UK Subs gigs.

He's certainly a genuine punk for how sullen and miserable he is and he never fails to emerge from his room without wearing his full get up (except for the slippers – bless him). But he's given up drugs and drink-ing and hardly goes out so his life consists of sitting at a kitchen table in silence eating toast and working his way through a vat of filter coffee. He fascinates me. What is he thinking about all day every day as he stares into space?

But he does say a few words to me. He wants to banter about the punk scene in London. I wish I could comply but I never know what he's talking about. 'I'm amazed!' Anja says. 'Raybay hardly says a word to anyone. No less in English. He must like you!'

'Great.'

The whole place is other-worldly to me. I've fallen out of my city-boy-nine-to-five routine and into this surreal combination of sounds, smells, lights, colours, sex, slipper-wearing punks... There's a huge basement cellar which mazes left and right, and up and down. Belé, an aptly-named humungous Brazilian with a humungous afro has a percussion band that plays gigs around the city. They often rehearse down there. Their rhythms resonate throughout the building (and yes, most men in the Bowles do have untrue-sounding names that consist of two rhyming syllables).

Everyone spends most of their time in their own parts of the Bowles. Anja has a large room on the third floor of the southwest corner, shares her bathroom with three girls and the large kitchen downstairs with eight people. Her room is filled with plants, yellow and orange are faintly printed on the white walls and thick tussles of ivy hang outside her window making the sunshine dappled and the rain patter sonorously.

We ignore what time of day it is and stay in bed. She fetches *Dreikornbrot* with jam and coffee in little blue cups when we're hungry. Dreikornbrot is a hard heavy bread, comes as a small, thinly-sliced loaf, isn't as tasteless or hard as pumpernickel, and it's typical of what Germans might have for breakfast with cheese or jam. I see Raybay eating a sandwich with pumpernickel filling – a bread sandwich. Kudos! Dreikornbrot and black coffee, for me, sums up Berlin; so dark, so hard, so bitter, so morish, taken with a sugary spoonful of something colourful to help it go down easier.

It takes a few days of shagging before Anja asks about me.

'What about you?' she asks.

'I spend a lot of my time in an office,' I say. 'For a year and a half I've had an admin job. Mostly I bind training manuals. I emailed them to say, sorry I didn't come in to work and I hope they can manage without me. They said they hired a temp and he's doing fine. Didn't take much effort to replace me.'

'That's sad.' Anja says. 'But the work sounds like it's soul destroying. Is that what you want to do?'

'Well, I try to write.'

'Really?! Write what?'

'Novels. I paid three hundreds pounds to do a correspondence creative writing course. They give me assignments. I mail them in, and they say they're all 'very good', along with a few spelling corrections.'

'Sounds like they ripped you off.'

'Well, it has got me writing. It's funny, that I have to pay someone to tell me to write.'

'Did it work?'

'It's made me write the first few chapters of my novel.'

'What's it about?'

'I don't know. It's set in a bar, and there are some people. Nothing much has happened yet. I just hardly have any time to work on it. By the time I finish at the office I'm brain dead.'

'I love that you want to do this,' Anja springs up from her lying position. 'You know, you could live here! You wouldn't have to pay any rent. You would have all the time you wanted to write, all the time that your art deserves, be inspired by Berlin, you can even learn some German.'

'What?'

'You're the kind of person this place likes to support. I'll clear it with the house and you can stay here with me.'

'Are you asking me to live here with you?' Bless her open heart.

She shrugs, 'Yes.'

'You hardly know me.'

'Yes,' she insists dramatically. 'I do.'

'I'd disappoint you.'

'You could never disappoint me. It's so nice to be with someone who doesn't recognise me. Everyone thinks they know me...'

It takes a supreme effort not to roll my eyes. 'It must be tough,' I say.

She asks, 'Does it surprise you that I was single?'

I say, 'Erm... sure.'

14th March 2005

I book a return flight to London to sort my life out. When I'm there I pack a couple of suitcases to take back to Berlin. My flatmates say they'll be able to find someone for my room in a couple of days. They're too busy for a goodbye drink as I didn't give them enough notice; pretty much sums up London-existence and Berlin starts to look more and more like a good idea.

I tell my plans to Mum. She cries. I give her a hug. I didn't realise the admin of leaving London would only take a few hours, and now I'm stuck at Mum's for two days watching television. The same people are having the same conversation on *EastEnders* as they were when I last saw an episode three years ago.

16th March 2005

I'm back!

And it feels amazing.

Anja seems happy to see me. We go drinking in Nollendorfplatz to celebrate (Christopher Isherwood's haunt!) which turns out to be two minutes from where we live. We arrive back at the Bowles at dawn and I'm slicing some Dreikornbrot wondering how I ever lived without this stuff.

And then things get weird.

We've had all night to talk, but Anja chooses this moment to drop not one, but two bombshells.

'God, I still have to pack,' she says. This isn't the bombshell, just the lead up to it.

'Pack for what?'

'I'm leaving for Cologne in a few hours.' That's the first bombshell.

'Cologne? Why Cologne?'

'I'm going to be in *Tatort*. Two weeks' work.'

'What's *Tatort*?'

'God, really? It's the most popular police show in Germany.'

'Two weeks? Today? That's crazy. I don't know anyone else in Berlin.'

'You can get to know people in the Bowles.'

'Get to know people?' I say, horrified.

'It's the plenum tonight. Everyone will be there. It's perfect.'

'What's a plenum?'

'God, really?'

My first morning officially living with Anja and I discover a habit that makes me want to scream. I don't know something (because, hey – I've never lived in Germany before) and she looks at me with large disbelieving eyes like I'm moron.

Yes! I really don't know what the fuck you're talking about, I don't scream.

I take a breath. I say, 'Really, what's a plenum?'

'The Bowles meets every week to discuss the house.'

'Every week? What's there to talk about?'

And then comes the second bombshell.

'Well, you.'

'Me?'

'You have to ask if it is ok that you live here.'

My stomach lurches. 'Are you joking?'

There's that look again. Eyes wide. *You moron. How could I possibly be joking? This is Germany.*

I don't scream. I say, 'I thought living here was all sorted, that I had 'Guest Status' and could focus on writing.'

'Nooooo.' Anja is amused now. It's almost as irritating as the disbelieving-moron expression. 'You have to go to the plenum, tell them how you will be able to pay rent and how you will contribute to the house.'

'How will I *contribute* to the house? I have no idea. Like what?'

'Like you want to repaint the rooms, do handy-man jobs around the place, shop for communal groceries, be sociable...'

'Sociable?!'

'...Have people over for coffee and make parties. That is important. This is a community. But most importantly you have to ask if you can live here. They may not like it because you have moved in before you asked.'

'Are you joking?'

Moron eyes.

'But I'm in a horrible position. I'd never ask to live somewhere after I've already moved in! I wouldn't have given up my job...'

'I don't want to argue the day I'm leaving!'

'I thought I gave up my job for something. I gave up my flat. If I went back to London now I'd have to live with my mum!' The thought makes me dizzy for a moment. 'I thought everything was agreed.'

'You're upsetting me,' Anja says. There are tears in her dark eyes.

I let it go. A devil of a headache is setting in.

We snooze for a couple of hours

Then she's gone.

The plenum is usually a fortnightly meeting where all the housemates get together, argue, write everything down and don't really resolve anything. They continue well into the night, and at the moment, there are a couple of controversial issues at hand so they're running weekly. They haven't even met me yet.

I arrive on time at seven in the *Mecca Küche*, a huge multi-coloured open plan kitchen where Che Guevara and Bob Marley posters adorn the walls. All the chairs are occupied and I sit on the stairs that lead to an elevated part of the kitchen next to a woman with straggly blonde hair and the general look of the older German woman that seems to be the norm, an exquisitely fit physique and waist so thin it defies biology, and a face that looks so much starker in age for its contrast with the youthful body.

Belé's conducting this plenum, taking minutes, and it's late by the time he introduces the big topic. Me.

'Paul,' he says.

He looks at me.

So does everyone else.

I take my cue.

'Hallo. Um. Guten Tag. Ich bin Paul.'

'Yes! We know who you are,' Belé says dismissively.

I lapse into English. 'So... I want to ask if I can live here. Sorry that I'm here already before I asked. And I... can't pay rent straight away. So... Sorry about that.'

With all the time I had to myself, perhaps I could have come up with something better than that. Then again, I probably wouldn't have. Not much of a hand to play with really.

The discussion begins, in German of course. More and more housemates speak. After five minutes everyone is shouting at each other and I have no idea what's going on. My discomfort isn't helped by the hard step I'm sat on; and now I'm gassy and have to work on clenching my butt-cheeks throughout the drawn out, humiliating ordeal.

The argument is over three hours long.

I later discover what the argument consists of; it isn't the first time somebody has tried to enter the Bowles in an underhand way; then again, I've been straightforward in the way I've introduced myself and stated my situation.

Finally, thankfully, everyone is exhausted, the discussion dies out, and the woman next to me leans over smiling and says in heavily accented English, 'Is good. Is all ok.'

'Great,' I answer, though my emotions have long ago slipped off to bed and I no longer care.

'Is important that you are sociable, have coffee with people, help with building, cook dinner for people.'

'Sounds nice,' I say, and it mostly does, except the whole forced nature of it all. *Be nice and sociable, or we'll kick your arse out of here.*

'So now, for example, I need help with my curtains.'

'You need help with your curtains?'

'Yes, because you are tall.'

'Oh, I see, help putting up your curtains. I'm your man.'

'Yes. Come with me.'

I realise she means right now.

*

Her room is half the size of Anja's, on the first floor of the northeast corner. I stand atop a ladder, on my tip-toes and hang her floor-to-ceiling curtains, and admire the ornate mouldings on the ceiling. These Berlin *Alt-Bauen* are insanely beautiful. And the woman chats affably... about the Bowles.

Then... I'm wondering how I can politely leave when she reaches up... and puts a hand on my inner thigh.

Her hand is on my inner thigh...

She's... putting the moves on me!

I flush at the boldness of it all, and steady my breathing so not to fall off the ladder in shock. It's not every day a guy is on the receiving end of this kind of thing, in my experience.

When I carefully step down, I receive a serious look from the woman with straggly blonde hair, a look telling me I'm about to get it. This is the point of no return. Am I going to make a run for it? It seems so impolite. Or am I going to sleep with a woman I don't even find attractive just because the opportunity's presented itself?

What about Anja?

Indeed, what about Anja? A memory plays in my head of her telling me to quit my boring life and come to Bohemian Berlin where free food and shelter await. And what do I hope is going to become of this relationship? I'm twenty-three and I guess Anja's somewhere in her thirties.

Straggly-haired lady takes my hand and leads me to her bed, then methodically undresses as if she's just got home from work. I've never been involved in such formal foreplay before, but I do the same. Her skin is bleach red from too much sun and vodka, so hard and rough in comparison to the woman I've been whispering sweet nothings to for days.

Anja.

I can't do this.

I open my mouth to mumble some kind of excuse but with a surprising swift motion and brute strength, straggly-haired lady grabs my hair and pulls my head down for a violent kiss, and uses the other hand to pull me down and inside her.

23rd March 2005

From the very next afternoon, a routine emerges. I'm invited for dinners and coffees and drinks by the Bowles cougars, and they talk about the Bowles like it's the only subject in the world (I suppose people can get locked in their own little worlds), and then they go all quiet and smile at me and touch my hand, and my arms end up around their thin waists.

I should charge considering I need to make ends meet somehow.

None of them seem interested in *me*, so self-absorbed in their actions and introverted in their orgasms; it really is like providing a service. 'It is really the best exercise one can do,' one says. Along with let-it-all-hang-out nudist culture, they really do know how to take the sexuality out of sex.

I don't know if they discuss me or compare notes but the method of seduction becomes so formulaic; after a few days I end up being the one to start the physical side of things to avoid learning more about the inner workings of the Bowles. I wonder if I surprise any of them who genuinely just want to have coffee with their new neighbour.

Today it goes off script. The boldly named (and married) 'Purificacion' is a Mexican woman living with her new and not so charismatic German husband. A dark-skinned, dark-haired beauty, she leaves me a note in German saying she wants to see me at three p.m. in her apartment. I translate the message with the aid of a dictionary, and when I arrive and knock on her door, she calls, '*Entrar!*'

I enter.

She is sitting in a chair, and she is completely naked. Well, not completely naked. Parts of her are obscured by the large cat she is stroking in her lap.

Do I regret my actions? I do. It's tough to look at yourself and not be the kind of person you'd care to shake by the hand. You'd rather put your actions out of your head as if they were the actions of someone else. I have some theories. I grew up a romantic. Then after years of teenage yearning, I finally nabbed a girlfriend, who I was with for two years. My first *girlfriend*. My first *love*. This was it – I thought. We'd stumble through life together like the lifelong partners in movies and sitcoms, and that was that.

But over those two years, this *love* of mine changed from a shy, friendly thing, into a beast. She yelled, she scowled, she was always angry, she cried when things didn't go her way; and just when I thought things couldn't get any worse, *she* dumped *me*!

So perhaps that experience destroyed any ideas I had about true love, and now I don't like to make things too complicated. We live for a short time so why pass up any sex-type opportunity? Anything Anja doesn't know can't hurt her. In a hundred years we'll all be dead, so who cares? Am I right? Or maybe I'm a dick. Maybe that's the danger with settling for someone you don't *love*; or maybe it's the more desirable option than actually caring properly about someone and being the one who gets hurt.

28th March 2005

I get a fittingly just reward. On what turns out to be my last indiscretion, right before Anja's return ... how do I put this? If you use something too much, it breaks. Mid-intercourse with Heike (from Stuttgart), a sharp shock of pain shoots through me. I make a puppy-yelp, pull out and grab my penis. I have no idea what's happening, but I do know there is a relentless gush of blood pouring onto my hostess's sofa.

The blood... is coming out of me!

I squeeze the poor chap, trying to stop the ejaculation of blood that's squirting everywhere, and Heike takes my arm and guides me to her shower. The gushing finally reduces to a trickling, and I cup enough water onto the chap to see that the join between my penis and foreskin has snapped.

The damage looks permanent. Jesus, I'm petrified. It's the end of my sex life – and I was just getting started! Heike is saying words like 'surgery' and things like 'let's show the other men in the house and see what they suggest you do.' I'd rather stay celibate for life than look into either of those two options. She takes pity on me for the undoubted look of sheer horror on my face and suggests taking me to a doctor. I wrap the chap in enough tissue so he's as snug as a package from Amazon.com, pull my trousers on, and we walk up Bowles Strasse for several minutes to the clinic.

The doctor is smarmy and condescending, but he puts my mind at ease, saying it will eventually heal, then he charges me a whopping eighty euros for the privilege.

30th March 2005

I decide to stay in the Bowles and wait for Anja's return, to tell her to her face what's happened. The least she deserves is the privilege of kicking my arse out onto the street.

She returns and seems very happy to see me. I get a hug and a kiss. Then she asks, 'How are you?'

'Well, not so good,' I say. 'You see, I've damaged myself.'

'What?'

'I've damaged myself. Here.' I point to the chap.

'How did you do that?'

I decide to attempt a lame lie, though arguably it's more plausible than the truth, especially to anyone who knew me in London. 'You know... when I'm alone... I....'

After a lengthy pause, Anja says, 'Masturbate?'

'Yes... a lot.'

Anja nods, eyes on the chap. She doesn't look disbelieving. I'd been all ready to pack my bags and be sent away. The best I was hoping for was not to get a shoeing in the groin before being shown the door.

But Anja nods. 'I suppose you were thinking about me.'

'...Sure.'

'I can understand it. I shouldn't have left you for so long. It's my fault.'

'Well, I didn't want to go pointing fingers, but yes, it's all your fault for being so beautiful.'

She loves that. She wraps her arms around me and presses against me, which sends serious screams of pain through me.

'Ow! Anja!'

'Oh, right, sorry.'

'It's really painful if he grows, then the wound breaks again.'

'Oh my goodness.'

So my Berlin story is destined to be longer than one chapter, and on the very night of Anja's return, she has a gig in the Tacheles. I'll finally experience the *miracle* of hearing her sing. She has to get there early to prepare, and I arrive later with a couple of housemates from the Bowles. They have to pay an entrance fee but I'm on the guest list. The man on the door doesn't look very happy about that. He wouldn't be happy about letting anyone so uncool inside, no less for free. But I'm Anja's boyfriend, the housemates tell him, which they all share a confused look over, like they're wondering, *what is she thinking?*

What *is* she thinking? One theory occurs to me: she's getting older and her beauty's fading, so she imagines a naïve youth from North London a safe bet, or a way to hold onto her disappearing youth. I don't know.

Everyone's confused except for Anja, who seems assured and confident in all her actions.

I don't do myself any favours by confidently striding to the bar, looking at the beer menu and loudly ordering a *Berliner Weisse*. That sounds like a solid manly Berlin beer, doesn't it? I'm given a red drink in a wine glass with a straw. Take a photograph.

So it turns out, a *Berliner Weisse* is a light beer which you have with a shot of raspberry or something green, which the French Huguenots concocted when they emigrated here in the seventeenth century. Even the drinks have a story.

I yearn to communicate with the affable group surrounding me but I can only stand around with an idiotic smile on my face. I'm introduced to Anja's number one fan, a woman who genuinely thinks she's the greatest singer of all time and never misses a gig.

She's tall and slender with the same delicate features as Anja, but more weathered.

She's an intense woman who packs a whopper of a first impression: 'Paul! Guten Tag. I know who you are. I am Franka, Anja's mother.' And two minutes later, '...When lovers left me, Anja felt that *she* was being rejected by these father figures, so she always tried to be the most beautiful, the best singer, an actress on television... Anja feels she is living in my shadow so she uses sex a lot to define herself away from me. She's very sexual. I'm sure you will have a very nice time.'

Yes, intense.

And with her delivery there are lots of pauses, and lots of staring, like she too is trying to decipher what Anja sees in me.

Franka pulls me to the front of the crowd, and Anja smiles at me while she sings and I have to dance with my big fake goofy smile to show them all what a good time I'm having. Anja does have a great voice and can really hit the top notes, and she's such a natural on stage. The crowd love her and dance hard. I'm drenched in other people's sweat and am very uncomfortable with the 'free' style of dancing. *Whoo! Let your body move however it wants to! It may make some strange shapes and unrhythmic movements but go with it!* A little self-awareness people, please.

I subtly drift away from Franka, then I turn and escape out of the bar area and into the stairwell.

Now I've finally lost my babysitters, I relax and take in my surroundings, and I'm in awe. The building is like an old ruin. It's cavernous, broken, scarred with old bullet holes. But there's art everywhere, wooden carvings, metallic sculptures, bright acrylic paintings on large canvases...

I head up the stairs admiring the broken plaster and peeling paint, the faded blues and dingy greys, I love the colours of this city. I wander around the top floors, find a mellow bar with a view of the city, a small cinema with oversized velvet chairs; and loads of empty rooms, a band rehearses in one, a couple of others are taken up by necking teenagers. I find exhibition space and grungy artists' studios with a laidback atmosphere – they work away while you wander in and out of their space, their pieces are available to buy.

I descend back to the ground floor and exit the back way. A surreally vast empty space stands before me. Half a car sticks out of the ground. Metal sculptures are scattered around. It looks like a workshop in a waste dump, though with a lot of very hip young folk laughing, drinking bottled beer; lots of colourful bulbs and fairy lights wrapped around trees; fires in steel drums, a Vietnamese man walks from group to group selling cheap beer and an old lady collects empty bottles to claim back the fifteen cent deposits.

I'm lost in the scene before me. Then a ball of fire blows in my direction and I stumble back like an idiot. It dissipates, its source a menacing steel dragon's face.

A girl in rolled shirt-sleeves gazes at me amused. I'm really epitomizing the stumbling Englishman that night. I attempt to save face with a little banter. I summon all my wit and come out with, 'Wow. Pretty cool.' Very smooth.

She's on her own, looking ahead and people-watching like me. She takes a drag on her cigarette and exhales. 'Thanks.'

'Oh, it's yours?'

'Yes.'

'...Do... you have a studio here?'

'Yes. Well, more like a little room with a bed and some materials.'

'You *live* here too? Amazing.'

She shrugs, 'It's open twenty-four hours, so I have drunk people banging on my door in the middle of the night.'

'Oh right, that doesn't sound so great.'

'No, it is great. This place is an institution. They say it will be gone this time next year but they have been saying that forever.'

'Why would they tear down such an interesting place? It's beautiful, it's good for tourism. What will they put here instead? Another generic restaurant and hotel?'

She shrugs again.

I grill her about the building's history. She speaks with an affably modest air, as opposed to the hot air my housemates riotously spout in the plenums. I notice her uncombed sandy hair and freckled skin, and her luminous blue artist-eyes. She has the amused grin of a happy child. She stumbles on her sentences, her German accent thicker than Anja's.

'Tacheles' is Yiddish for 'straight talking'. The building was originally a department store in the Jewish quarter of Berlin. It served as a Nazi prison, then a travel agency, and a school. It deteriorated and further demolition began in the eighties. Then two months before the planned detonation, an 'Artists' Initiative' moved in. Now there are art studios and bars, and a little arthouse cinema at the top. They really do put English squatters to shame.

I'm about to ask blue-eyed artist girl her name when Anja is suddenly standing beside me rolling a cigarette. 'Hey baby!' she says territorially, staring daggers at the other woman.

I'm about to make an effort at some kind of introduction when we're distracted by a pub crawl – it's the same company who were dragging me around when I first met Anja. What a crazy coincidence. I'm about to point this out when there's a loud cacophony of chants and laughter. Two of its members stray to a far corner for a shag. Actually I'm being kind, there is no corner. They've just walked a few steps to where it's a bit darker. A crowd surrounds them. The couple carry on humping. The crowd cheer them on.

Then they're done. I imagine a moment of clarity will hit them and they'll stand, sober and shame-faced. But the girl curtsies and the guy takes a bow. The crowd applaud and she says in a thick Essex accent, 'It's alright! I'm English!' Cringe.

Anja is looking at me. 'I'm of Italian descent,' I tell her.

The band members are a sweet bunch. They love the fact that I'm English and want to rap at me or have me read and check their lyrics. Most German bands perform in English which I find strange. We all walk along the river to Bar 25 and only then do I realise I've lost the blue-eyed artist girl. Shit. Ok, it was a brief encounter but something felt… so natural and right about it. I'm irritated she'd been scared off. I'd nearly made a friend.

We skip the queue, standing along a high wall, and enter another world. Our new venue is a Bohemian summer resort, hidden within a city that you forget about until the trains run overhead. Beautiful kids in sunglasses lounge around as colourful as jars of mixed fruit in the cool air of a spring night drinking on the riverbank. A crusty wooden shack shelters the bar. The sight is stunning in the twilight before sunrise.

And them, damn, I see the same sordid sight twice in one night. A gorgeous pair who look narcissistically like each other start getting amorous on the river bank. Then one is on top of the other. Then they're going at it. I say some disapproving comment to Anja.

'Oh. Don't be English and prudish,' she says. 'This is a city for lovers.'

I love that about her, her positivity, her inability to be judgemental, her – despite her age – youthful innocence. The world is a beautiful place full of beautiful people like her. She's… unspoiled.

At the same time I resent her for it. Everything seems to be so easy for a beautiful woman. Her mother had found her the spot in the Bowles so she'd had time and no financial worries while she worked on her art (rent in the Bowles is amazingly cheap). Elusive fame that most people dream about just happened to her — she sang in a band in school and got a record deal. The same with falling in love, it doesn't occur to her that most people make faces at our age difference. Even I had been easy, a boy who never thought he'd leave London; she said she wanted me and I dropped my life to join her, not even sure if that's what I want to do.

Anyway, enough about my issues and back to the shenanigans at Bar 25, Mr and Mrs Narcissus are so hot and heavy they slip off the side of the bank and into the river. Everybody cheers. The couple climb out, the boy remounts, and they start up again.

'Ok,' I say. 'They get kudos for that.'

Anja looks at me like the cat with the cream. She wraps her arms around me whenever she has the chance, and even though the party shows no sign of slowing down, and we're not able to partake in our favourite hobby, she says she's desperate to take me home and have me to herself.

We get a taxi at Jannowitzbrücke and share it with Max, the drummer and manager of the band – a gorgeously handsome, sweet-natured guy, for part of the way. 'He's so nice but can't find a girlfriend who's nice to him,' Anja says.

So why didn't *she* go for him? I don't understand it.

And we arrive home at the Bowles. I don't understand this either. How have I suddenly come to live in this unusual timepiece? Our home's grand interiors, deep greens and reds, and heavy beaten-up furniture are right out of a Christopher Isherwood story. Whispers and heartbeats linger from the past. As Anja leads me by the hand up the sleeping stairwell, I have to wonder, how many lovers and affairs has this museum seen? And how many of those lovers had completely screwed everything up by sleeping with half the female population of the Bowles?

We lie by candlelight. Anja asks hopefully if we can attempt to do *that thing*. I see my own frustration in her eyes. This woman who people desire as she struts on stage is wholly mine. Other men's advances only irritate her. But lying with her in the half-light, I'm effectively impotent.

Anja has a large library and asks if there's anything I'd like to have read to me. The idea of being read to is a strange one. I shrug and say, 'I don't know.' She's not dissuaded. She opens a bottle of wine and reads me some Erich Fried – an Austrian poet who fled to London and settled there after the Anschluss – in the hope I'll 'find it inspiring.' She reads the German, then the English. It's very beautiful and simple.

I already mentioned the appeal of her voice; words travel to me as smooth as thick spoonfuls of honey, and my hand rests on her creamy thigh. What did I do to deserve this lovely moment? I decide, I should be a very good boy from now on; but this relationship is surely doomed after all I've been getting up to. It would be a matter of too little too late.

I hold her close and she looks at me with tender eyes. I have an overwhelming urge to tell her how I really injured my member, and I have to work hard to summon my rational self who says: she's not *the one*, there's no such thing, she's someone you are sharing this moment in time with and she seems happy – that's all that matters, so why spoil it?

If karma's waiting before dealing its decisive blow, for now it's smiling at me mockingly. I desire her with my entire body... well almost my entire body. When our lips touch I can feel blood pounding powerfully through me. My main tool of desire throbs painfully in protest and threatens to break. Teeth and eyes clenched, I withdraw from her warmth and drink another glass of wine.

Night becomes day, which turns to night again. We lose all sense of time, and talk and read, and I explore her body with my eyes and fingers. I've never felt closer to anyone. Without *that thing,* and without the mundane nine-to-five routine I've been a slave to all my life, we go to a place I've never been before. Things are getting complicated. After sabotaging everything in such bastard-like, dramatic fashion, I can feel myself falling in love with her.

14th April 2005

'I thought we would get to know each other in the sauna.' What a clichéd, schoolboy fantasy it is to hear those words. And from a sexy older woman. But they are said to me under circumstances that give me no schoolboy thrill.

Anja's mother says this to me. In front of Anja. And the rest of her family.

I don't immediately panic. My subconscious clasps at irrational straws. 'The sauna' is probably a trendy Schöneberg café?

Don't be stupid. This is Germany. More likely we're going to be sweating in a room together.

Then stepfather-Wolfgang tells me, 'Katja was too young before, and too shy to come into the sauna with us with Anja's new boyfriends, but she is mature now.'

Now I'm sensing, not only will there be no coffee and cake, but there may be no towels or swimming costumes either; this is a butt-naked thing.

I'm dreading the thought of seeing Anja's family as it is, the intense mother, the stepfather who has single-handedly landed me into a pit of debt, and there's a sister too, what does *she* have in store for me?

We meet at Bülowstrasse station. I shake hands with Wolfgang – the stepfather, Franka – the mother, and

Katja – the beautiful younger sister. We make a quirky group. Franka is twelve years older than Wolfgang and fifteen years older than daughter-Anja. I'm a little older than Katja. But wait for it. I was at a party with Anja recently and a guy bluntly asked her how old she was. She hesitated, then answered, 'Forty.' That makes her three years younger than her step-father and seventeen years older than me!

But things haven't begun to get weird yet.

We enter a strange factory complex, and up some stairs to arrive at *Sultan Hamam*, an 'authentic Turkish Bath'... and into the unisex changing rooms. That old Monday-morning-swimming-lesson-dread I had as a kid, when I was certain every week I'd drown, twists my stomach.

My new adoptive family start throwing off their clothes with ease and I try to look as nonchalant.

But I don't feel nonchalant. My unsightly balls itch. My flaccid penis flaps to its own tune, and without the cushion of clothing, wiry black hairs grate my jaundice-coloured skin. I'm tall and keep a beard because of the boyishness of my face, and I have broad shoulders, so clothes hang off me well. The rest of me is knobbly, and hairy where it shouldn't be hairy. I always avoid seeing myself naked and I don't think anyone else has seen me properly starkers at all before I came to Berlin. Talk about the deep end.

I take a deep breath and tell myself to deal with it. A friend recently told me a similar Brit-abroad story. She was at a friend's house and the family had invited her into a hot tub. Her advantage was, she wore glasses. All she had to do was take them off and everything before her was a blur. How I wish I could have gone back in time to yesterday – I would have jabbed myself in the eyes until I needed glasses.

The experience is a funny one, for the mix of the eroticism of the female form and the comedy of the male. Anja, Franka and Katja drop and step out of their skirts – such a natural movement – while Wolfgang and I struggle, pulling our trouser legs away from our ill-shaped limbs.

The bodies of the three women emerge, as fresh as milk and roses. I look down so as not to leer at them in awe. But then there are so many naked men, a wall of German male flesh, a haze of hairy legs and arses exposing themselves with guile, flab hanging at strange angles the way male physiques awkwardly do.

I keep my face fixed and expressionless, though I feel a lot of conflicting emotions. I'm told we'll have our own private room and I'm not sure if that's good or bad news.

Katja is Anja's half-sister. She looks strikingly different. Anja's hair is thin and brown. Katja's is thick and blonde, its waves caressing her naked back as she walks in front of me to our room, close enough to reach out and touch, and while no one can notice, I drink in as much of her as I can, like a naughty boy carousing his dad's glass of beer behind his back.

Franka is an older version of Anja, and she has something about her that makes it obvious she's a passionate and sensual woman; maybe it's the fact that she's as hot as a Carolina Reaper chili pepper. She shares the same penetrating green eyes as Katja. The identical attribute on all three are their smooth youthful shoulders, surreally lined up in a row; I don't know if we're purposely seated by our sexes, but Wolfgang and I are sitting on too-hot benches in one corner, and the women opposite. I can't deny how grateful I am for the seating arrangements, three wonderful women with perfectly rounded breasts and formed hips sit before me.

The three women seem cockier than when dressed, excuse the term of phrase, surely aware of the excitement they're arousing. They start talking to each other in German so unfortunately I have no excuse to look at them.

Wolfgang speaks to me with his little member sticking out from under his fat belly, scratching himself at me, void of any shame or self-consciousness. And I try to be affable and listen but can't get over my dislike for him. He's been a catalyst in my dream move to Bohemian Berlin turning into a horrific series of unfortunate events.

The Wolfgang situation
I haven't written about the Wolfgang situation yet, so here it goes. It begins in the Bowles. After a night at Silberfisch, we return home and I slice some *Dreikornbrot* to soak up all the raspberry beer I've been drinking. (I

keep forgetting not to order Berliner Weisse. It's such a normal name for such a weird beer!)

I try to chew the impervious bread and a tooth in the back of my mouth shatters. Crunch. Anja's laughing so hard, tears roll down her cheeks. 'Zat is zo funny!' (She sounds more German after a few drinks.) 'You are so stereo-type-English! With your bad teeth, and your soft bread which you can squash and it becomes half the size! One bite of real bread and your tooth is broken!' Considering the pain I'm in, her laughter's in bad taste. Quite irritating actually, but she makes up for the performance by taking me to her dentist in Potsdamer Platz the following morning.

Potsdamer Platz is an impressive sight, and a surprising one, being at the top of our quite ordinary street. As we walk north, the modern landscape appears on the horizon, with the newly finished roof of the Sony Centre designed to look like Mount Fuji.

Potsdamer Platz was a bustling metropolis of casinos and cabarets, and the film-making centre of the world in the 'Golden Twenties', where Fritz Lang filmed *Metropolis*, before the Nazis took over UFA to make their propaganda films. In the Film Museum that now resides there, you can see a picture of the vision Lang created for his masterpiece, with bizarrely shaped buildings and futuristic art deco design – probably inspired by Potsdamer Platz, which claimed to be the busiest crossing in the world at that time. Next to it is a picture of the Platz today (after thirty years of being an empty death strip that divided East and West Berlin during the days of the Berlin Wall), with its large overbearing angles and dominating corporate headquarters, that seem to be inspired by Lang's vision. Life imitating art, imitating life! It's not a popular place with most Germans as it cost many hundreds of thousands of euros per square metre to create and lacks any sense of heart or soul.

But more impressive than the sight of Potsdamer Platz is the sight of the German dentist. My experience of dentists is waiting in a room that looks like someone's living room that hasn't been cleaned since the eighties. Well, it usually is someone's living room that hasn't been cleaned since the eighties. This place has a reception, and the dentist actually has an assistant. *Two* people attending to *my* teeth!

The *Zahnärztin* (female tooth-doctor) explains and Anja translates that it seems as if I've never had my teeth professionally looked at before (and they both laugh) and that I need costly root canal surgery, so I should get my medical insurance sorted before she did anything.

'Haven't you got your medical insurance yet?' Anja asks me. I don't even know what medical insurance is, coming for the land of the NHS. Medical insurance? Damn, I've never been to a doctor in my life. Now I'm falling apart.

The two ladies talk and come to a consensus. The dentist sands down the sharp bits of my broken tooth so it doesn't cut into my cheek and, Anja explains, we need to sort out my insurance before I get any more treatment. Her stepfather is an insurance man and he'll sort everything out.

I'm a lucky boy.

Or so I think.

I swear, I speak to Wolfgang over the phone later that day and he says to me, 'You do not have a job. Because of this you do not need to pay for your medical insurance.' He takes my details and that week I get my first monthly bill demanding I pay two hundred euros.

I panic and immediately call Wolfgang. 'Of course you have to pay,' he says to me.

'You said I didn't, because I don't have a job.'

He laughs. 'Of course you need to pay your insurance.'

What is up with this family? First I'm promised free accommodation, then Anja doesn't know what I'm talking about when I repeat back to her what she told me, then this. And the cherry on the cake is, when the date of my surgery comes round... my expensive health insurance... doesn't cover dental, so I don't get my tooth fixed, but I've managed to acquire debt. Rimshot, please.

So no, I don't participate in much conversation with Wolfgang, and the rest of the family eventually help out by switching to English and conversing with us. We talk about the Bowles of course. There's always some 'interesting' bit of Bowles gossip or politics worthy of discussion.

Actually, one genuinely sad thing *has* happened concerning two girls who live in our part of the building. Carla, a girl in her late-twenties, who smokes a lot of weed, who has an obsession with Reggae music and Jamaica, has lived in the Bowles for a good few years.

Jarral, a younger, more timid German girl, who has an obsession with Brazil (she loves everything, the music, the flag, the language; she works in a Brazilian café, plays in Belé's band... and yes, it's strange the women in the Bowles all choose a specific country to become obsessed with) has moved into the Bowles only recently.

Carla adopted Jarral as her little sister and took her to clubs and parties. Jarral made the mistake of dancing with a guy Carla had her eye on. Carla didn't say a word and showed no outward signs of hostility, but when she left for a four month trip to Jamaica, she sent an email to everyone in the Bowles saying she was vetoing Jarral's request to live there (every new housemate has to have a three month trial before becoming a resident in the Bowles, and every resident has the right to veto).

But dancing with a guy is not a fair reason to veto and kick someone out of their home. But a veto is a veto. But Carla just lazily emailed her veto and isn't making herself available to discuss it. But a veto is a veto. But Jarral is just about to complete her three month trial and everyone likes her, and she has nowhere else to go, and isn't the whole point of the Bowles, is that it doesn't deal stoically with rules, bureaucracy and bullshit and the residents pride themselves on having the freedom to talk things out as opposed to saying, a rule is a rule and nothing can be done about it? But then again, you know what they say about vetoes.

So the family discuss this and I roll my eyes because the Bowles is all I ever hear about. Jesus, living there can be such a pain in the arse. Sure, it's cheap and funky, but it's a full time job. Home should be where you leave all your troubles of the day behind, not have a weekly all-night plenum to hear people shout for and against Jarral and Carla.

I'm growing drowsy in the misty air. The Germans get to talking about the party the Bowles is throwing for its twenty-fifth Anniversary, and without realising, I start saying how unsettled I am by all the preparation I've been involved in: '...I mean... *organise a party*. Doesn't that seem strange?' I go on to make some fantastic generalisations: 'Germans seem to have a lot of *control*. Even when they're having a party, they're not going crazy – there's *control*. I walked into a bar the other day and was asked for a small cover charge...' and I put on a German accent for this quote – perhaps dazed from the heat, or the embarrassment I'm feeling, '*Because vee have made a party, zere will be some nice music and a buffet...*' And we went to *The Long Night of Museums*, free buses are running every ten minutes to take you around the city, guides are there to show you around all the exhibitions...'

'So what's your point?' Franka asks me.

And I say, 'It's like they've analysed what makes a good time and executed it to the smallest detail, and everyone has their fix of fun and goes home contented. I mean, even the graffiti here is neatly done.'

'So you're saying, even when we party, we are like Nazis?' Katja says. She has an American twang in her accent, I guess from all the American media we all consume.

I don't know what the hell I'm saying. We're all naked for Pete's sake. When I don't answer, Katja continues, 'I know what makes me content so why should I put up with anything else? If the most important thing to the English is beer, why don't they sell nice beer there? I went out with people in England one night and one guy said...' and she puts on an amusing cockney accent, *'I'm gonna get shitfaced then I'm gonna have a fight! Is that normal?'*

She is so confident in her glorious silky bareness, and her aggression results in an unusual flutter between my legs. Oh god, no. I haven't been embarrassed by an inappropriately timed erection since I was a teenager who used to get aroused on bus rides and had trouble standing at the end of a journey. I struggle to think up something unsexy, and I wonder how many naked arses have sweated where mine is sweating now. This helps.

'I think we *are* very controlled here,' Anja defends my comment. 'And that's because our grandparents *were* Nazis.' Our eyes meet. Anja isn't going to be outdone by the sexiness of her younger sister. She has a wistfully admiring expression on her face that I wish I could freeze-frame and keep. I'm guessing she finds it endearing, how squeamish I look, and she understands why I've been rambling some silly unclear opinion.

'And we're not allowed to forget it,' Katja says. 'From the moment we're in school, we're told we suck.'

Did she say *suck*? Ooh err.

'It's... not as bad as all that,' I say, needing to stay in the conversation now to have something serious to focus on. 'I'm British. Our history's just as dark. We created concentration camps too.'

'People are proud to say they're part of the British Empire or Commonwealth or whatever it is. You don't know what it's like being German. Everyone calls us Nazis. We can't so much wave a flag at our own football matches.'

'Well it's a pretty ugly flag,' I quip. I guess I like it when she's angry.

'We need to talk about your prejudices,' Franka says sternly, like a very, very sexy school teacher. Oh dear. I'm not prepared for that, and I feel that inconvenient flutter again. She gracefully leans on one arm with her legs crossed, wiping the dripping sweat from her shiny moist thigh, her shiny glistening sweaty thigh. It strikes me what a perfectly erotic word 'thigh' is, the way you have to raise your tongue to your top teeth and begin releasing your breath over it, following up with an almost mournful sigh.

In my desperation, I stop breathing. That doesn't help the situation, and I subtly exhale cold air through pursed lips, managing to desist the old chap. All this time I'm being spoken to. They're awaiting an answer. I attempt a non-committal, 'Hmm.' It sounds more like a moan.

At least things can't get any worse, or so I imagine. Perhaps to change the subject, or to make me seem less prejudiced and more comical, Anja decides to tell a story.

'It's hard to start a new life in a new country. Poor Paul is stuck in the Bowles with a load of boring Germans. Then I had to go to Cologne for two weeks. He spent so much time on his own, he constantly masturbated and injured his penis.'

I lose the ability to breathe for a moment, but then I'm surprised that the family are amused. They laugh, as if this was a normal, amusing anecdote. So I'm able to collect myself and I assume my idiot's grin.

They get into the topic of conversation while I keep on bearing it and grinning.

So they have a reason to look at me but I'm not allowed to let my polite field of vision stray. This isn't fair!

'How did you injure your penis?' Katja wants clarification.

'Masturbating!' Anja confirms in a *I-know-it's-crazy!* tone of voice.

'Wow. How much do you have to masturbate to injure your penis?'

'A lot,' Wolfgang explains.

'How often do you do it?' Franka asks. Franka is my girlfriend's mother by the way. And she's asking in all serious curiosity.

I choose a convincing number. 'Seven... times a day, while Anja was away.'

'He is young,' Franka states.

I feel low and degraded. Can I just pack in this life of a clown and go back to England though I've given up my job and life there? I can't screw or chew. I've moved into a house of thirty non-English speakers who I can't communicate with. I doggedly try to learn German words and conjugate verbs every day while everyone rambles incoherently around me. The German language itself is more frustrating than anything else. I mean, a dozen variations of the word *the*? And what are separable verbs all about? Splitting a word, putting half of it at the beginning of a chapter and half at the end? You need a maths degree.

I'd also hit the low of working for a telesales company for three days, on commission of course (i.e. for free) before deciding it was futile. How am I going to make this work? How could I have forgotten how impossible it is to get a job and the promise I'd made myself that when I did find one, I'd keep a firm and desperate grasp on it for the rest of my life? I'm eating into my English overdraft and my bank is sending me letters enquiring why no money is going into my account. With those two-hundred-euro insurance bills about to pile up every month (which even though they don't cover my dental, Wolfgang insists I have to pay by law as long as I live in Berlin), debt is about to take on a whole new meaning for me.

'Don't you see that is the problem of English people?' Katja is saying. 'You turn your sexuality onto yourself, and you do yourself harm. English people are still living in the Victorian times. You know, before you had Queen Victoria, English people were like the Germans. Women showed their ankles, there was nude sunbathing...'

'I don't know about that,' I say, for lack of any other generic comment.

'It's true!' she says angrily, and my heart thumps loudly against my chest.

'She even changed the names of streets because she found them upsetting. Like 'Petticoat Lane' in Spitalfields became 'Middlesex Street'; and though she made homosexuality for men illegal, she didn't bother with lesbianism, because she didn't believe something so lewd could ever happen...'

She continues to vent. I wonder what her point is supposed to be. Does me injuring my penis have anything to do with my being English? It's unbearably hot. Katja is unbearably beautiful. My brain is melting. The air pummelling me into the floor. The humiliation of my own nakedness is just... awful. Tears of sweat sting my eyes and I have to squeeze them shut. A vision of Katja walking towards me...

I force my eyes open. And I nod like I'm listening.

'...And you are the one talking about control,' Katja concludes. If only she knew how much control I'm exercising she'd cut me some slack.

I stare laboriously at her face as she speaks.

But I'm occasionally treated to a glimpse of the upper part of her chest.

As her breast rises and falls with her breath.

Then, as if working in cahoots,

Franka stretches,

Arching her back

And letting out a sigh.

And I am gone.

I'm not strong enough to fight it.

There is nowhere to hide.

I'm swollen with fantasies,

Rising

As fluids well up inside me.

Wolfgang laughs. 'You're looking very comfortable, Paul!'

The women aren't so amused, wide-eyed at the most riotous hard-on I've ever had.

5th May 2005

Nollendorfplatz
Altbauen – beautifully décored and restored
Red-brick churches
and small intimate cafes
surrounding a gorgeous market square
This is where I live
My neighbourhood
So full of colour and life
The layout, the architecture
So pleasing to the eye
I just sit here people-watching
I could sit here all day every day

It's not just Anja I'm falling in love with. It's damn fine living in Berlin. You can cycle to work on the wide empty roads (Berlin's population is a third of London's), cruise across the city in twenty-five minutes or contact a friend at short notice to get ice cream on a Sunday at midnight in a café on a cobblestoned street. (I don't have a job or friend – but it's all potentially there for me.) At the foot of most apartment buildings are all night restaurants and bars, so the streets are always lit and inviting.

I grew up in Harrow, where grey skies, concrete buildings, and cracked tar roads full of traffic dominated the landscape. I feel like I need to sit here and absorb all that's around me in my new home to feel human again after years of living like a cog in a badly-oiled machine.

This is Nollendorfplatz, the centre of gay and Bohemian life in Germany during the Weimar period between the wars with its theatres, clubs and cabarets. Despite the Altbauen, I feel no sense of history sitting in its cafés. It's fresh and new, with its curry houses, sushi restaurants, cocktail bars and young people. But this is where Christopher Isherwood wrote his famous *Berlin Stories* which became the film *Cabaret*. Some internet research led me to Fraulein Thurau's boarding house on Nollendorfstrasse where he lived, worked and set his stories. This was a thrill as I'd been getting my pizza slices from the amazing Dolce Pizza stall just two minutes away nearly every day. Imagine: 'Where is that place that I want to go pay homage to? Oh, two minutes down that street.'

Isherwood arrived in Berlin in 1929 to visit his friend W.H. Auden and ended up staying until the Nazis were in power – burning books to send a message to the rest of the world about what they stood for. His writings sum up the vibrant Weimar culture that existed before Hitler. It was a time of decadence and dancing while the Nazis lurked menacingly in the background – they were actually comical to the Berlin hipsters, handing out propaganda flyers and asking for donations. And as they seized control of Germany, Berliners became even more party-crazy, as what else is there to do when the world seems to be coming to an end?

When Anja and I need a break from each other, she has her friends in the Bowles to have coffee with. I head to Nollendorfplatz to drink long glasses of *Weissbier* and people-watch. (Yep, I've finally learned to stop ordering Berliner Weisse – I'm practically a native!)

I've just received another useless insurance bill I can't pay, been demanded rent I don't have, and my tooth and other injury are gently throbbing. Nursing a beer and smoking a cigarette on Nollendorfplatz, I can't say any of those things are worrying me.

As they methodically repair all the buildings in Prenzlauer Berg, they tend to leave one on each street as it was, scarred with war and left alone during the time of the GDR; but Nollendorfplatz is pristine, a place you can go and forget that you have any troubles, or that any exist in the rest of the world. It doesn't even get overcrowded, the twice-a-weekly Winterfeldtmarkt has just the right amount of people sampling coffee and buying flowers and cheese. It puts me at ease to sit here, I do so for hours.

Perhaps when you choose to lighten up and not worry, the universe smiles on you. I hardly know a soul outside of the Bowles, but a warm shadow falls over me and I know its owner. A quick smile and the lightest blue eyes I've ever seen; I can place her immediately.

'Blue-eyed artist-girl from the Tacheles!' I say rather too excitedly.

Her eyebrows crinkle at the title I've given her.

She's holding a pad to take my drink order and damn am I pleased to see her. I have to confess something at this point. Have you ever made eye contact with someone on a bus or the street and feel as if your paths were supposed to cross? Of course it would be creepy to say anything and you both continue on your own paths and one day you realise years have passed but the image of that person is still engraved in your memory.

I didn't know her name, and we only had the shortest of chats before Anja circled us like a cat to pull me away, but she was never far from my thoughts. She was like a marker. I wondered if I'd ever bump into her again, what she'd think of the progress I'd made in the city, my improved German and knowledge of Berlin. And I'd laugh at myself, wondering why someone from such a random meeting would stick in my head so much. I always wondered what she was doing and yes, I knew she was living in the Tacheles so I could have tried to find her, but I chose not to, allowing her to live on in my mind as the girl with the loveliest smile whom I never saw again.

She recognises me and we chat for a long time despite it being her shift. She is so easy-going, so cool. After a couple of hours the bar is less busy, and she sits with me, not talking, just people-watching and sharing her cigarettes.

*

I tell her about my time in Berlin (not how I've creepily kept her in my mind and often toyed with the idea of trying to see her again) and she listens contentedly. Boy, I haven't met a listener since I arrived in this town.

'So where are you from?' I ask.

'Berlin.'

'You say that like I'm supposed to be impressed.'

'You are.'

'I'm not.'

'Aren't you?'

'No. I think it's quite pathetic actually.'

'I suppose it is,' she says.

This is unbelievable. We're having banter. I haven't bantered since... I can't remember.

'There aren't many people here who are *from* Berlin. It's a new city. It's still being built. Industry is yet to arrive. People who want a career or a serious job generally go somewhere else. Then, people who aren't from Berlin are coming here because it's an exciting place to do something different; new enterprise, art, or...' she gestures at me, 'be a professional relaxed person.'

'I think it suits me.'

'It does,' she says, flirtatiously?

I become awkward and blab anything. 'So... you say, Berlin is 'new'. What was it like before?'

'It's always been quirky. Before the Berlin Wall fell, West Berlin was the only place in West Germany where you didn't have to do military service, so this was where all the punks and the like came to... play.'

We have a couple of beers together (on the house! If I'd have come to Berlin to be with this lady, I wonder how different my financial situation would be). I'd already had a couple of beers, and beers in Berlin are half a litre, so I'm feeling pretty good about the whole situation, and blue-eyes suggests going to a place in Prenzlauer Berg. I text Anja that I'm tagging along with some types I've just met, and we take the U-Bahn eastward.

As we walk, she turns to me, smiling. 'I'm Pat.'

Pat takes me to the *Weinerei*, a large café with a mix of worn-classical and wine-crates-for-chairs décor, next to the autumnal coloured Zionskirche (Church of Zion). With the ancient, period furniture, the thick, velvet curtains and patchy lamplight, it's from another time.

We drink wine together for ten hours, then walk up the tower of the Zionskirche and see an awe-inspiring view of the city.

Pat looks at me.

I look back at her.

After we look at each other for a long time, she asks, 'How is your girlfriend?'

'Fine,' I say.

19th May 2005

The sombre cosiness and cheapness of the Weinerei has lured me into a ritual of leisure, wine and coffee every day. What a place. The lone chef – quiet, moody, skinny – works miracles; fresh, sweet and savoury pies, filled croissants, and two vats of exotic soup with chunky pieces of bread provide the aroma of fresh cooking. A buffet is laid out in the evening and it's never ordinary, there are strawberries in pasta dishes, peach and beetroot salads... he's a genius. An odd thing about the odd-looking chef is I often see him in the most random and far flung places around the city, sitting on a kerb, alone, doing nothing. Very mysterious. I wonder if he's not of this world.

After eight, you pay one euro for a glass then pour all the wine you want and help yourself to the buffet, and you pay what you feel like when you leave, a typically bizarre Berlin enterprise.

I don't know what would have become of me if I hadn't discovered this place. I've been living off communal groceries, Anja's food and leftovers from people's meals in the Bowles, and reading Isherwood was the closest thing I had for company. You can't have a drink at the Weinerei and not strike up a conversation with whoever's sitting on the wine crate next to you.

But Pat is my number one. She lets me whine about my troubles and she's helped me, by putting me in contact with people who can help me out finding work teaching English.

For a few euros we get fed and merry. It's a simple, hand-to-mouth existence and I feel I've earned these hours of leisure, my cheap glass of wine and my plate of pasta after hours of bluffing English in a classroom. ('Why do we say *pair of trousers*? Because... in the old days, before central-heating, Englishmen would wear *two pairs* of trousers and for some reason we still say *pair of trousers*.')

Surrounded by cigarettes, wine and blurred conversation, I know I've arrived. We gather around a large picturesque outside space half way up the hill and if it rains, we huddle in the loud rooms, dense with smoke and damp with sweat.

And Pat tells the greatest stories. Every time I see her she has a hilarious tale from the day.

One time, she'd just come from her kickboxing club, and one of the trainers brought his little boy in who would run around annoying everyone. He took a long run and barged into a big punching bag which flew up, back down, and knocked him off his feet. The boy landed on his arse and starting wailing, and Pat couldn't stop laughing. Everyone was looking at her, and the trainer was very irritated at her *Schadenfreude*, while he tried to comfort his child. And Pat tried but she couldn't stop laughing, same as me as I listen.

Another time she got into trouble with the *Polizei* for smoking weed on the street. She put on a charming smile and pleaded something to the effect of, 'Come on! Is it so bad? Go to the Weinerei and everyone is smoking out in the open!'

'Yes!' answered the Polizei. 'But *you* are standing directly outside the police station!' She throws her head back and laughs, and it's so adorable something in my heart twists every time.

And this is a great story, and I'm actually with her for this one. After a session at the Weinerei, we think about renting a film and go into a video store. For a laugh, we go into the *backroom*. Backrooms in German video stores are insane. It is wall to wall, ceiling to floor... porn, and they're always bigger than the normal, front part of the video store it's attached to!

And what porn!

The most graphic, most violent, angriest, rape-iest stuff I've ever seen. I'm not saying I've seen so much... anyway...

(By the way, on the subject of the sex industry, Pat tells me there's an eco-friendly brothel in Berlin where, if you can prove you've ridden your bike there instead of driving your car, you get a discount!)

Anyway, the punchline of this story is... Belé, the Brazilian housemate, is there. Not only is he there but he's holding an explicit DVD in his hand. Not only that, but Pat – after I explain who he is and why we're staring at each other awkwardly – goes to him and says, 'Hallo.' She takes the DVD out of his hand and says, 'What are you getting? Oh! *Slam it in every hole*! Good choice!'

My eyes close and when they open, all I can see is Belé's face, and it looks as if he's going to pull a gun and shoot me in the head. Pat hands back the DVD and we shuffle out.

'What were you doing?' I yell.

'I don't know. It just happened, I guess, because the situation was so awkward.'

'So you decided to make it a hundred times more awkward?'

Now she can't stop laughing, and now neither can I.

We walk down to *Slumberland*, the bar she works at in Nollendorfplatz where we'd had our reunion, and laugh like annoying people who laugh a lot in bars, though not without a sense of trepidation in my gut.

I tell her about Belé. He's such a dominating character, a huge man who takes up all the space that surrounds him in every way. 'If anyone says something at the plenums and he disagrees, he just shouts them down with his booming voice and gets his way. You know, everyone has to do a three month trial before they get to live in the Bowles permanently. He's the only person who didn't have to do it. Just talked over people and bullied his way in. You can tell when someone brings it up, it's the only time you'll hear him laugh awkwardly as he changes the subject.'

'Did you do a three month trial?'

'I'm officially just a guest at the moment, but I'll have to do it eventually. Anyway, Belé has this ownership issue with all the young women who live in the Bowles. Anja told me to watch out for him; he's very weary of any boyfriends they might have.'

'Yeah?'

'Yep. Once it got back to her that a guy she really liked asked if she was single and Belé threatened him to leave her alone.'

'*Scheisse*! She should have done something.'

'Like what? He's a scary guy. I got a similar story from Simone, she used to live on our floor. She had been single and lonely for a long time, so she was over the moon when she met a nice guy. Belé and Simone were close – she played in his band – he shunned them, spread rumours, told them separately how they weren't suited, he kicked her out of the band and generally made life so impossible for them that she left the house after years of living there.'

'How close were they?' Pat asks. 'Do you think he loved her?'

'I don't think it was like that. It's just about control. I mean, get this, he's got a wife. They're not separated, but they don't live together. Apparently she's got lots of money. She comes to the Bowles sometimes dressed very elegantly and they act really warmly to each other.'

'How do you think he'll act when you see him next?'

I drain my beer.

21st May 2005

I don't see Belé for two days. I try to go about my normal routine, though my heart skips if I'm ever in the kitchen and someone enters. I hope to be in a crowded room when I do see him, then I can give him a smile and a reassuring nod before he delivers any threats, a nod that communicates, 'Hey man, it's cool, we're *guys*, we all want to *slam it in every hole* sometimes.'

Alas I am alone in the kitchen helping myself to a slice of someone else's cheese when the door flies open and *the presence* enters.

After recovering from the shock of the door crashing against the wall, I'm poised to grin and nod but he stops me by pointing a threatening finger at me. His eyes are wide with danger and his whole, huge body is clenched like a fist. I put down the butter knife and prepare to dodge him. What's he going to do? He moves slowly and comes in close, towering over me. He says in his deep voice in broken English something to the effect of, 'If you want to stay here and live in this building, you have to do the three month trial.'

'Yes, I know...' I begin.

He cuts me off with the finger. 'If you do, I will make veto, and you'll have to leave.'

23rd May 2005

I meet Pat at Slumberland at the end of her shift and we drink beers outside on a warm summer evening. For some reason she's wearing a long black coat.

I tell Pat what Belé's said.

In her lovely way, she can only laugh. 'Why does he hate you so much?'

'I don't know. He must be really embarrassed. But Anja warned me; it's an alpha-male thing. He doesn't want another alpha-male in the nest.'

'But you're not really an alpha-male,' Pat says.

'...thanks.'

'What will you do?'

'Well, I still have 'Guest Status'. A couple of people have mentioned I'll have to eventually do the trial, but I'll just keep smiling and avoiding it and I'll see how long I can last.'

'You're going to let him push you out of your home?'

'Of course I am.'

'Well, we should get drunk.'

'Sounds like a plan.'

'What do you want to do?'

'I don't know... buy wine and watch a DVD at your place?'

'Come on, don't be boring. It's Tuesday night.'

I shrug and ask, 'Any ideas?'

'Yes!' Pat slams down her beer glass and says, 'Let's go to the Kitkatclub!'

'Sounds good,' I say. 'Do they have kit-kats?'

'No, I came up with the idea when you were talking about that English writer who lived in Berlin. I watched *Cabaret* and everything happens in the Kitkatclub.'

'It still exists?'

'Yes! Well, no, it's a bit different. But it's basically the same idea. You said you wanted to go somewhere dark and seedy.'

I had mentioned to Pat that I'd been disappointed not to have found any cavernous bars in stone-walled cellars. Such Gothic settings seem to be a thing of the past in Berlin. I hesitate, 'I... did, but maybe on another night when I can build myself up to it.'

'Come on. Are you a mouse or an alpha-male?'

'Something in-between?'

I'm nervous but I accept the challenge. We make our way south of Schöneberg. And then – as is becoming the pattern for me with ladies in Schöneberg (ok, we're closer to Tempelhof, shut up), Pat reveals a weird, sexual surprise.

I thought she had been wearing more make-up that usual – she doesn't usually wear any – but this evening her lips are moist and blood-red.

Well, under her coat she reveals she's wearing a PVC costume which shows plenty of cleavage and just about covers her arse, and fishnet stockings. There are also knee-high boots with spiky heels that I could have noticed earlier but I guess it's obvious at this point I'm not one to pick up on things like what shoes people are wearing.

I catch my breath and state the obvious, 'Erm, Pat, you're dressed like a dominatrix.'

Pat smiles in her girlish way and says, 'It's a fetish club. They don't let you in unless you're dressed up.'

I shiver at the thought that Anja had been really close to joining us that evening. I'd told her I was going for beers with my new friend, and she said, 'That's great! Where shall we go?'

And I hesitated, '...Well, the thing is. I'd rather it just be me and Pat. I only have this one friend. You're in a house full of friends and this is my only chance to get away. Wait, that sounds terrible. I mean, I want to keep this friend for myself. For now. That sounded bad too.'

So I was about to change my mind but of course Anja said, 'No! It's ok! I want you to have friends outside the Bowles. Though I'm curious what he's like now!'

And I had to say, 'Well, Pat is short for Patricia. It's a girl.'

'A girl?' Anja's smile disappeared.

'Well, she's like a guy. She drinks more than I can.'

I'd got defensive. Anja gave me an intense stare, and I kept an expression of upmost innocence. But I'm not innocent. I know I must be hurting Anja. Pat and I are seeing a lot of each other and I'm happy to have an excuse not to see Anja on stage all the time. 'Oh... your gig is tonight? Damn, I already told Pat we'd go to this thing. I hate to let her down.' And now I'm looking at her dressed up for a night in an S&M dungeon.

I say to Pat, 'Is there something you're not telling me about you?'

Pat giggles. 'I don't usually dress like this, I swear, it was you who gave me the idea.'

'But I won't get in. I'm not dressed up. I'm in jeans and a T-shirt.'

'But it's ok if you *dress off*,' Pat experiments with English word-play.

'What do you mean *dress off*?'

'I mean, if you *dress off* to your underwear they'll let you in.'

'But isn't this weird? We're friends and we're going to go into a fetish club.'

'Come on. I always wanted to go in here but didn't want to go on my own. Think of it as fancy dress.'

And I do. What the hell. I have the courage of the Dutch, and I'm wearing clean underwear... I strip to my boxers and trainers (removing the socks as I don't think that's a good look), and in we go.

The techno is thumping. Through a vibrating swirl of reds, pinks and sparkles, I see a blur of leather, corsets, bare breasts, rockabilly hairstyles, metallers, shaved heads, all types, all ages; and people dancing together and groping each other and they are just fabulous... and some quite ugly. A few men are just topless or in something tight, and a few women aren't dressed so outrageously, well, they'd probably turn heads in a 'normal' club. A handful of men have got in looking ordinary like spoilsports at a Halloween party, and that makes me wish I had something to spice up my look. I almost ask Pat for some eyeliner but... I don't. There are some beautiful dancers, and the older people celebrating themselves in their funky outfits are awe-inspiring. To think that when Anja took me to the sauna I'd been ashamed of my young physique, which is only going to deteriorate as the years go by.

I just about manage to contain myself despite all the attractive women in body stockings and bikinis surrounding me. I'm dizzy and realise why I'd been reluctant to enter (ok, it doesn't sound like I was particularly unwilling to go inside, but I'd put up a bit of a fight). The truth is, I'm scared of myself.

I think back to the mixed feelings I'd had in the sauna I'd had to share with Anja and her attractive sister and mother. Now I understand things better; I sense a nasty seediness inside me that I mustn't release on an underworld like this. Others may be embarrassed, amused, willing to try something new, or perhaps feel happy they've finally found where they belong. I feel... a pleasant darkness. I'm *too* excited about the idea of going into a fetish club with a pretty young thing who isn't my girlfriend. Get through tonight in one piece, I tell myself, then never come back to a place like this.

In some ways, the club isn't so sleazy. You get worse nights in your local Wetherspoon's. People are dressed strangely, but there's no aggression. In fact, I'm the most aggressive person in there, as I drunkenly trip into a group of people standing at the bar.

I drunkenly apologise and one of them manages to give me a quick snog before I slip away.

Two topless women in burlesque outfits dance on the stage. Pat and I get a drink and take a seat to watch the show. A bluegrass band start to play a set and a stripper appears in corset, Venetian mask and a feather boa. She moves slowly and smoothly, twirling and moving her hips left to right hypnotically.

Then her hand moves to her vagina and she pulls out a streamer. Pat and I raise our eyebrows at each other. The streamer turns out to be very long, and she times it so it ends with the song.

Applause.

I turn to Pat, 'So is this what you had in mind?'

She seems miffed.

'What's the matter?'

'Some people are dressed quite normally. I didn't need to dress up like Elvira.'

'So what? You look great.'

'You think so?'

Uh oh. Where's this going. 'Sure. You should dress like that more often.'

'I'd probably get better tips.'

Phew. Situation avoided by use of humour.

Then Pat says, 'And I want to see people having sex!'

'People just start boning in here?'

'That's what I heard.'

She looks around and I take the opportunity to look her up and down. I'd had the impression she'd be wiry but she has a lot of nice curves in a lot of nice places. My head spins like I've just taken a drag from a too-strong spliff, and I escape to the bar and start buying us both shots. I hope I get her drunk enough so I can take her home before something weird happens. I think that's my plan.

I realise how drunk we both are when we think we're about to set our glasses onto a table, yet they end up smashing on the floor instead of getting anywhere near a table. And I just want to reach out and touch her even more. I buy a round of tequila; Pat gulps it down gratefully, and says, 'Thanks, I needed some water.'

We're too drunk to get up and dance so despite the extremely alternative setting, Pat and I end up doing what we do every other night we hang out, smoke, drink, and watch and comment on the people around us.

'I'm starting to get it,' I say to Pat.

'What?'

'This, the German nude culture; the wild, arms-flailing dancing... There's no bullshit. I went to *Fabric* in London one time. It's pretentiously expensive. Everyone there does these same mechanical dance moves because if they look different to anyone else, they're a freak. No one can see or hear anyone else and they all face the DJ making it all look like an army drill.'

'I heard it's a good club,' Pat said.

'There's just so much hate in there, and I immediately lost my friends when we went inside and there was no phone reception so I couldn't find them again and so I just people-watched. I saw one guy purposely sidling left to right so someone would bump into him so he could get into a fight...' I see Pat is listening intently, but now she has one leg hanging over the side of her chair. Quite a sight. I've lost my train of thought. I say, 'I'll get another round in.'

I try to stand, and I have to sit back down. I take some deep breaths, and suggest, 'Shall we head off?'

Pat looks disappointed. 'I want to see someone *doing it* first!'

'There's a guy over there masturbating. Does that count?'

Pat seems to seriously ponder this, but finally decides... 'No.'

I find this hilarious and am unable to swallow the beer I've just caroused (possibly someone else's beer at that). I'm left with my cheeks puffed with drink, and Pat takes the opportunity to slap me on both cheeks, and she's somehow shocked when – surprise, surprise – she's sprayed with two cheeks of beer. We both find this hilarious and my sides hurt from the laughter, then we're embarrassed to discover *we* are receiving strange looks from the people around us.

I plead. 'Seriously, the room's spinning,' and she helps me up and to the door. We're on our feet, holding onto each other. I look at my legs, it helps to keep moving forward; it keeps me steady somehow.

But then the floor starts slipping away.

So I say, 'Screw it!' If the floor isn't going to stay in one place, I'm going to grope Pat.

I grab her breasts as the room tilts on its side, and we fall onto a wall. We kiss like we're trying to eat each other's faces. She reaches into my pants, where my hard-on isn't hard to find, and wraps her legs around me.

We look at each other with orgasmic O's on our faces. She squeezes me between her thighs until it hurts and I dig my nails into her buttocks and she bites my ears... and it doesn't take long.

And of course, with the aftermath comes that moment of clarity: *I just had sex without my girlfriend – which I PROMISED myself I wouldn't do again because I LOVE her – in a club full of people and I want to get out of here... but I probably have to share a cab home with this 'friend' and it will be so awkward... and I've ruined this amazing new friendship...* I look at Pat's face, expecting a look that mirrors my feelings, or a post-sex-sentimental smile; but she's laughing, so I laugh too. She says, 'Fuck, we better get out of here,' and we run from the spot like it's a *Tatort* (Crime Scene).

In the cab, I wonder if she'll nestle up to me or turn away, looking awkwardly out of the window, but I'm pretty lame at guessing whatever Pat's going to do next.

Her head lolls back and she falls asleep with her palms facing upward.

I watch her. How does she manage to look cute and innocent, dressed like she is? I laugh at the memory of her drunken announcement, 'I want to see *people having sex!*' That really sums her up. She doesn't take life seriously. The things we do in life aren't carved in stone for people to tut at for years to come. I've always seen life as an egg-timer sitting precariously on the edge of a table – time slips away or it falls and everything smashes. That's probably why I do things so fast and lacklustre, including sexual relationships, wham bam, thank you ma'am, another experience notched up before nothing-ness takes you; a case of doing as much as you can in a day as opposed to making the most of a day.

Life is not dull around her. Being with her makes me less afraid of being alive, less afraid of dying.

The only sounds are the dance of other taxis.

The day folk are sleeping.

The cobblestone streets are silent.

I alone hear the call of the night;

Its hymn to love and sex and Patricia's thighs.

I swear

In this city of ghosts

Something is happening that has never happened before.

This old town hears words

It's never heard uttered before

I say to Pat, 'You are beautiful.'

Her eyes are closed.

Her sensual monkeyish lips are parted slightly.

I tell her, 'I love you.'

The motion of the taxi moves us along.

And I'm moved to my core that I can be so 'profound'. My eyes water with sentimentality. I take her hand in mine. She starts to snore.

24th May 2005

I promised myself I would never be unfaithful to Anja.

Again.

And I lasted a few measly weeks.

Actually my member had only healed enough (from the last time I'd been unfaithful) for me to be unfaithful again a few days ago, so if I was to replace 'weeks' with 'days', that would be a fairer assessment of what a shitheel I am.

After the tremor in the Kitkatclub and the earthquake of emotion in the taxi, Pat wakes up when we arrive outside her place in Mitte. She hugs me and says goodbye, smiling; no shame or sentimentality.

I ride back to the Bowles and drag my feet up the stairs. I'm looking forward to having a dramatic moment with myself in front of a mirror. I want to take a good look at the man who stares back at me and cast judgement, say to him, 'Who are you? What are you looking for?'

I have lots of existential questions brewing, but I only make it as far as the kitchen.

The light's on. Raybay, the Bowles's last remaining old-school punk, is sitting at the table smoking and drinking coffee. I guess he's been there all night and doesn't usually see other people at 5am on a Wednesday, and being caught off guard makes him unusually animated. His eyes widen and he asks in slow, broken English (which I transcribe here in plain English) something like, 'What are you doing up at this time?'

And though I write this in plain English, when I speak to him it's in a slow mix of simple German and English. I slump in a chair next to him and say, 'I had some beers with a friend.' I gesture to his cafetiere. 'Can I have a cup?'

He says, 'Sure,' and proceeds to ignore me.

I'm fascinated by Raybay, and surprised that no one else is. I ask Anja, 'What's his deal? How can he just sit in a chair all day not talking to anyone? Doesn't it drive him mad?'

The only answer I ever get is something like, 'I don't know. I don't give a shit. Why should I? He doesn't give a shit about anyone else.'

He continues to look at his coffee and I'm drunk enough that I can unselfconsciously study him. His stubbly facial features are squashed like a pumpkin. He has long dirty blond dreadlocks, and wears skin-tight flannel trousers that accentuate his skeletal legs. His costume and hair and piercings are the most striking thing about him, and only after a while do you notice how small he is and the lines on his face could mean he's as old as fifty.

Why would a man dress himself up in that get up? Isn't it impossible to pick up women? Whenever I watch people running to their jobs in uncomfortable shoes or around the park in their tracksuits, or looking miserable in cafés in uncomfortably tight hipster-outfits, I wonder if everything we do in our lives is about getting laid with the most attractive people possible. When people get married it must be because they realise they can't do any better. There's just nothing else. I mean, I loved art and grunge music and not washing my long hair as a teenager, but when I realised the girls at school only went for the generic types, I bought a plain shirt, had my hair cut like everyone else, stopped speaking my thoughts, and it worked. Since then the writing and drawing I did was always on the sly, only in Berlin are people more interested in that side of me than what job I do, or don't do, and it's with reluctance that I'm starting to open up about it.

Finally I've stared enough, and I look away and regress into a state of spaced out blankness, which is what I tend to do whenever I have a lot to feel or think about. Raybay seems to grimace with irritation at my presence, maybe thinking I'm trying to be sociable, but he eventually realises I'm happy to be quiet and sullen too and I can sense him relax.

By the time I've finished my mug of coffee I realise I must have been in a trance for a long time. I sigh and shake myself out of it. Seeing I've come back to life, Raybay says, 'Purificacion is looking for you.'

'Oh shit,' I blurt out. The woman whose idea of seduction was leaving me a note summoning me to her room, then waiting for me in a chair with her cat in her lap looking like a female villain in a Bond film. It *was* one of the most thrilling moments of my life but she scares me. I want these shenanigans behind me. That she's openly looking for me makes my stomach hurt. 'I think she wants to talk about the rent I owe,' I lie.

'I think she wants something else,' Raybay says, and he looks at me for a second, not smiling but with humour in his eyes. In that second I realise that though he never speaks to anyone, he listens; and he knows about all the things I've done since entering the Bowles.

I guess he's safe because he doesn't talk to anyone else and I feel stupid lying to him. I say, 'Yeah, I think you're right.'

We seem to have made some kind of connection and I venture a question. 'Hey, Raybay, what do you do?'

'As a job?' he asks.

'Yeah,' I shrug, as if to say, for starters.

'I'm a caretaker in a school,' he says, and I just assume he works part-time like everyone else in the Bowles. It's funny, I was often tempted to work part-time in London to have more time to write, but when I mentioned it, people looked at me like I was crazy. In the Bowles people work part-time and think the idea of full-time work is mad. Why would you spend five or six days of the week during the best years of your life working?

Raybay continues, 'I also restore furniture. I've collected all the furniture that's in the house.'

'What?'

'Haven't you seen my room?' he asks.

How would I have seen his room? 'No.'

'Come have a look.'

I'm expecting black walls, a dirty mattress and a roll of toilet paper. In actual fact, it looks like a furniture showroom; beautifully restored antique cabinets and tables, and he sleeps in a grand four-poster bed. Separated from his comfortable living area is his workshop. The only feature I see that I expected to find in a punk's quarters are the hundreds of beer bottles lined up neatly, each one with a different label.

'Strange to have all these bottles if you don't drink,' I say.

'I used to,' he says. 'They're German beers. I like it. It's no bullshit. Countries like America brew shit beer and brand it and export it round the world. Ninety-eight percent of German beer gets drunk in Germany. We brew good beer and we consume good beer. It's cheap too. Too good and too cheap,' he concludes.

I nod, getting his meaning. I'm continuing to transcribe an awkward broken English and German conversation here.

He also has a film projector and a huge collection of horror films. '*Do you like scary movies?*' he quotes a famous line to me.

'I like zombie movies,' I say. 'I guess I can relate to the brain-dead, coming from London.'

At the mention of London, Raybay grins a shy, quite pathetic grin with his eyes cast to the floor. He punches a fist in the air and says, 'Yeah! London! UK Subs!'

He suggests watching something and offers me a non-alcoholic beer. I'm exhausted but can't refuse. I assume I'm the first person to watch a film with him in years. The non-alcoholic beer tastes ok, and watching *Dead Alive* projected onto Raybay's wall is something.

*

After nine hours sleep and lots of vitamin C, I seek out Cat-woman. Knowing she's looking for me, I can't relax until I've faced the situation. Her apartment is on the second floor on the southeast corner of the building.

I stand outside her door, fear permeating my body and I want to get myself together before I knock, but she senses me and opens the door before I have the chance. She look *very* serious, it's a little emasculating. She tells me to come in, in a tone that says I've done something wrong and am about to be duly punished. With my smattering of German and GSCE Spanish we communicate on a basic level.

Cat-woman and her husband have really struck gold. This is the nicest space in the Bowles; spanning two storeys; large, bright and open, with exposed beams, divided by no walls or middle floor. They have a large bath tub, have built their own kitchen and have a door that leads directly onto one of the nicer garden terraces. It's all about timing in the Bowles. They haven't lived there as long as many of the other residents; they were in another space and when this one became available, they said, 'We're a couple and the space would be ideal for us,' and presto, ridiculously cheap, luxury living.

She's fully clothed, I'm relieved to see. Her diamond-shaped face is stunning and I feel faint just being near her. When she turns her back to me, I try not to, but I check out the curves on her figure. I have to put my arm on a table for support.

'Would you like a beer?' she asks in German.

'Ja, danke,' I say, though I don't want one, but it's comforting to have something to hold onto.

Our conversation goes something like this (I think): 'I have been speaking to Anja.'

My heart jumps. She can't have told her the truth, surely? She's being threatening but playful.

'Ok.' I nod.

'She said your little injury is better.'

'Well...' I want to tell her it's none of her business. 'Sure, it's better. I was worried...'

She interrupts me by coming up to me and grabbing my crotch. I try to back off but she's got a surprisingly firm grasp of my equipment.

'Things are different now,' I say. 'I really... love Anja. Now. More than before.'

'It doesn't seem like you care for her much.'

'I do. I have to start being a good boyfriend.'

'Take off your clothes,' she demands.

'What?'

'Take off your clothes,' she repeats. 'Or Anja learns about all the things you've done.'

'Seriously...'

'Do it.'

'Purificacion...'

She slaps my face hard.

'Ow!'

'Do it!' she demands.

This is great. I'm being blackmailed into infidelities so that my girlfriend won't find out about my infidelities, and I think I'm falling in love with Patricia anyway. Am I going to let some Bond villain do this to me? The thing is – well, one of many conflicting things is – Anja and our time together does mean a lot to me, and I don't want her to find out about the unthinkable things I've done, because that would make her feel like she's nothing to me. I *hate* being an adulterer. 'You've only got yourself to blame,' a smarmy voice in my head says. 'It's like the old saying goes: Careful where you dip your wick, because if you dip it in the wrong ink pot, she'll have you by the nuts.' That can't be an old saying. No old saying would mix metaphors like that.

While all this rambling is going on in my head, I've subconsciously undressed and am standing in front of Cat-woman with my arms by my side. I'm still in a state from the night before and feel like I'm having an out of body experience, watching the situation unfold from an armchair, and thinking the stance of the naked man standing before the Medusa rather pathetic.

She approaches me and pushes me back onto a kitchen chair. Boy, she is crazy. I think about her husband, such a small, softly-spoken, shy type; one of the few housemates who speaks English; he's always very friendly to me, often hinting that we should go for a beer together. The problem for me is, he's a bit too nice and quiet, and I'm often stuck for anything to say to him. How do you talk to someone who's nothing but nice all the time, and how does he handle this maniac?

I realise I've been hand-cuffed; my hands are locked behind my back and to the chair. Gone is my last chance to run away, but that would mean telling Anja... then where would I live? The Berlin dream would be over, and how would I go on seeing Pat...? My mouth positions itself to let out an angry curse but I manage to stop myself and I calmly plead, 'Cat... I mean, Purificacion, seriously, what would Josh make of all this?'

She walks away and stares at me from a distance. 'I want to look at you like this for a moment, all tied up and helpless. That's exactly how I want you. Hey! Look at me, boy! You're enjoying this, aren't you? You like a woman to tie you up and tell you what to do, don't you?!'

'Um, not really.'

'You want it badly, don't you?!'

'Erm, I don't know. Want what exactly?'

She undresses slowly and part of me rises to attention. She stares with an expression of satisfaction as she approaches, her feet patting the floor. Then she's standing over me. I swallow. She positions herself perfectly and comes down hard, taking the whole of me inside her.

'Wow,' I yelp, amazed not only by the sensation but her skill.

She absolutely rogers me. One long fast deep thrust after another. Ramming me down onto the chair so hard I fear we'll crash through the floorboards.

She mouths nasty low whispers. I think she may be praying until the words become loud enough to hear. 'There was a boy like you in school,' I think she is saying from my limited Spanish. 'The quiet type, always sitting at the back, watching everyone...' Her sentences are interrupted by her grunts and moans. 'He never spoke to anyone. He used to walk around like he was better than the rest of us...' She caresses her breasts. I don't want to make a noise and press my lips together. 'I thought he was handsome and I'd wear pretty little dresses and I would smile at him shyly and he would never notice me...' The rest of the story escapes me and I don't know what becomes of the boy I remind her of. Either he becomes a rich politician eventually arrested for corruption; or a bank robber who steals a lot of money and avoids capture. My Spanish is very sketchy.

I hold out for as long as possible, perhaps hoping I'll satisfy her and she'll be done with me, content with her conquest; but knowing from my expression that it will be over any moment, Cat-woman demands, 'I want you to cum everywhere.'

I try to nod but I'm bouncing so hard on the chair it doesn't show.

She slaps me again and demands an answer. 'Ok?!'

'Ow!'

She jumps off me, grabs my todger and shifts her breasts over it, and I cry with agony as her demand is obeyed.

Once I can see straight again, I see Cat-woman transformed. She is satisfied and resembles a human being again. She's wrapped herself in a dressing gown and smiles almost girlishly, unties me and kisses me softly. I kiss her back. 'Same time tomorrow,' she says.

'I, uh... have classes,' I stammer. 'I'm working.'

'When will you be free in the day again?'

'Um, next... Tuesday.'

'You'll be here at the same time on Tuesday then,' she states.

She disappears into her bathroom and I hear the shower. I use her tea towel to wipe any incriminating wetness away, dress, and get out of there.

30th May 2005

Now I'm in good working order again, and being blackmailed by Cat-woman to visit her at least once a week, risking getting caught and losing everything, the other cougars look scorned when I reject their new run of invitations for coffee. In fact, everyone in the house is taking a gradual disliking to me because of small incidents that keep happening.

For example:

One night in the Weinerei Pat says to me (so I believe), 'In Germany, we have the funniest show called *Stockenblocken*, where contestants have to pile bricks at perfect right angles, and when their minute is up, they bend all their joints at right angles!' Then she jumps up and into the right-angled stance of an Egyptian mural. It sounds hilariously stupid and I ask everyone in the Bowles about it but no one knows what I'm talking about.

So I look on the internet and as chance would have it, I find the clip I'm looking for just as a large group of people are passing my room and I tell them, 'Come in here! I found an episode of *Stockenblocken*. You have to see this! It's so funny!'

...And the clip begins, but it's not a German TV show. It's the *Conan O'Brien Show* making fun of Germans. Pat's

English isn't perfect and we have the odd misunderstanding. Conan O'Brien says, 'This is the kind of thing *zee Germans* watch on TV.' It cuts to a woman who is given one minute to put different objects on a table at right angles. When her minute's up, a man in an SS uniform measures everything with a set square, declares she's failed, then beats her to death. The camera cuts back to Conan, his American audience laughing, and he announces, 'Germans! They're so weird! That's what they call entertainment!'

So five German housemates are staring at me in disbelief and I'm not sure what to say. 'Erm, my friend told me about it and it sounded funny. I'm actually very offended by this! Because you see, I thought it was a German show... because her German isn't very good... so, you see? I thought it would be... different.'

Another time, Laura, a rookie German language tutor who lives in our quarter of the Bowles, very kindly offers to give me and her American friend, Julian, German lessons in her room. She's young but very serious, her dark hair always tightly tied back accentuating her pointed, mousy features.

In the first lesson, she says the German for 'the way' as in route is '*der Weg*' but 'the way' as in the method of doing something is '*die Art und Weise*' (naturally these phrases have different genders. I sigh, knowing how much trouble I'm going to have remembering these words, and scribble them down in my fifth, crammed

German notebook. That same lesson, we play a word game to help us remember vocabulary. Laura says (in German of course): 'I went to the shop and bought a kite.'

Julian says: 'I went to the shop and bought a kite... and an elephant.'

And I say: 'I went to the shop and bought a kite and an elephant... and a cup.'

We keep adding a word, trying to get the sex of the word right and remembering everything that's been said previously. After two and a half minutes it's getting tough and though I think I've succeeded on my turn, Laura says, 'You lose, Paul. You said all the right things but in the wrong order.'

I sigh, accepting defeat. 'In... the wrong... order?!' I say to repeat her German, then to repeat some other bit of German I've just learned, I say, 'That is not the German *way*!'

Laura looks stunned. She says, 'So the German *way* is to be very tough about rules because we are typically very efficient and like Nazis like in that video you showed everybody?'

'... No. I was just practising using the word.'

'You have no idea how much I get this from my English students...'

'It was a joke,' I insist.

'I know,' she says. 'You think I can't take a joke? Because I'm a typical German and Germans don't have a sense of humour?'

Apparently not. 'It was just the perfect moment to say *Art und Weise*...'

'I'm sorry,' Laura says, her voice cracking. 'But I haven't experienced a direct prejudice attack like this...' her raised voice trails off as her large husband enters the room.

Julian and I stand up.

'What's going on?' the husband asks, his eyes boring into me. (Not Julian, mind you, but me; good instincts!)

'We were just leaving,' Julian says, pulling me out of the room.

So after these two incidents, combined with the fact that my German is so bad it seems like I'm aggressively refusing to communicate, there's a general feeling in the house that I'm a typical English 'wanker'. They also drop hints I've had 'Guest Status' too long, but I avoid saying I'd like to do the residence trial, what with Belé's threat hanging over me.

But thankfully no one has the gumption to directly confront me about the situation, and I'm always smiling and pleasant to people, and I think I've become Bowles's longest reigning 'Guest', which is something. Also, everyone seems touched by my blossoming friendship with the unsociable Raybay, who's talking to me more than he's talked to anyone in years.

Anyway, none of this stuff really matters. What matters is, it's summertime in Berlin. The city is beautiful. It's hot and sunny every day. I ride a bike, that Anja gave me, everywhere. Every place is new and authentic. My favourite place at the moment is

Mauerpark and its weekly Sunday market, with all the strange bits and bobs being sold and the strange-looking folk selling them, and all the unusual musicians every few yards.

25th September 2005

Haven't had time to write in a while. A lot of teaching work has started to come in and I don't feel I'm in a position to turn any of it down, but it's so hard. I lied about my qualifications so it takes ten times longer to lesson-plan than it should. I swear, I was never told a thing about grammar at school. English is English, people just speak it! I wake early to get to class, then finish the day exhausted. I come home and go straight to bed for a nap. Then it's near impossible to get back up to do my homework before the actual time I should be going to bed for a night's sleep.

I'm constantly bluffing when I'm asked questions. 'Do I say 'which' or 'that'? 'Maybe' or 'perhaps', 'the group *is* going' or 'the group *are* going'?' 'Why do we say 'I forgot *to cook* something' but 'I lay *watching* something'? Is it 'I started to panic' or 'I started panicking'?'

I don't know! I don't even know how to say 'gerund'? Is it with a hard or a soft 'g'?

Now I'm earning some money and no one has told Anja about how I wore out my member, maybe I'll get to stay in Berlin, maybe it will become sustainable. What I'm earning is a fraction of the insurance debt that's building up against me. My only hope is if I ignore it long enough it will just disappear.

Pat and I never talked about what happened that night in the club, and I'm worried I missed a window to be more than just friends with her. She doesn't act differently. She is always herself. So I never said anything. We continue to hang out and get drunk together. And now she's started to talk about other guys to me, as if I'm some kind of... friend. So great, we're in friends-territory.

Autumn has begun. The colours in the parks, like berries, hay and freckles, are wonderful. The musicians in Mauerpark wear gloves with the tips cut off so they can play their instruments while protecting themselves from the bitter cold.

27th September 2005

It's Friday evening. I'm sad I'm aware of what day of the week it is again, not very Bohemian. I'm battered after a week of intense teaching. Anja's going to band practice like she does every Friday night. It's an annoying time to be left alone every week, but Pat calls.

'I don't know if I like you spending all this time with your pretty friend, Pat,' Anja says.

'Do you want me to sit around on my own on a Friday night?' I say.

She can't argue with that.

Pat's starting a new job in a gallery tomorrow, so she wants a quiet night in with her boring English friend. I find the prospect quite exciting. 'Great! We can cook together, maybe watch a film...'

Belé's been in the kitchen all day preparing the mother of all space cakes. He grows a lot of cannabis plants; you can find them in different locations around the Bowles. Not only does the cake contain an insane amount of weed, but instead of using flour, he's using dried shredded leaves of the plant.

I'm curious about it and ask Anja to get me a slice before she leaves. She comes into the room with a tiny slice. It tastes like chocolate cake, and I decide to leave the last morsel; Pat can have it when she arrives.

When Pat's here, Belé's no longer in the kitchen, and we set about making some dinner. Pat sits at the table watching MTV and I get busy at the stove pulling out pots and pans. I absentmindedly remove every pot and pan from every cupboard. I have no idea what I'm supposed to be cooking. There are a lot of communal goods at the Bowles bought from a kitty that everyone contributes to, so there's always everything from toilet paper, toothpaste, tea, herbs, garlic, onions; and potatoes and pasta that I'd made great use of during my pre-teaching days.

I collect every communal item of food in the kitchen, then I go round the house collecting all the pasta and potatoes I can find from every other kitchen. I put everything into four large cooking pots. There's no serving dish large enough to maintain the mountain of pasta and potatoes I've cooked so I find two large buckets to serve them in.

I place the buckets on the table. Pat gives me a look, and I realise what I've done, and we burst out laughing. Then I sit down short of breath and I can feel my skin melting. I take some deep breaths. The feeling only gets more intense. Blotches appear in front of my eyes and I start to panic. I get the sweats, I feel sick from my stomach to my skin, and I'm sure that if I'm in this state, Pat surely must be having an awful drug experience. I swallow my pride and say, 'I don't feel well, Pat. How are you?'

'Fine.' She smiles. 'I'll take a potato,' she says comfortingly, plucking a potato out of a bucket and biting into it.

'Pat! Are you sure you're ok?'

'I'm fine,' Pat insists. 'I'm happy just watching MTV.'

Ah, so she's watching TV to distract herself from the bad trip she's having. I try to do the same but it doesn't work. 'Pat, I'm sorry, I have to go and lie down.'

She raises her eyebrows in concern. 'Are you serious?'

'Just leave everything here. I'll tidy up later.'

'Are you ok?'

'Ugh, no, maybe you should go.'

'What?'

'You'll need someone with a key to let you out the front door; there's always someone around.'

I get up and feel my way up to my room. In bed, I start fearing for my life. I'm practically convulsing, my leg kicking out repeatedly. I'm scared I'll forget who I am and I repeat my life facts to myself. 'My name is Paul, I live in Berlin, I'm feeling very intense because I ate some space cake.' I can't tell if my eyes are open or closed because all I see are dark blotches.

Pat comes in. 'Paul, are you ok?'

I focus my mind to tell my leg to stop kicking out, and manage to say. 'Sorry about this, Pat. I have to go to sleep.'

'Jesus, I'd be worried about you if I didn't know it was just a bit of cake.'

'Yeah, I just need some sleep.'

'Paul, there's no one around. I can't find anyone to let me out.'

'Sure there is. There's always someone. Anyway, you should sleep here,' I say, thinking she must be feeling at least something like what I'm feeling.

'No, I'll go, but you have to let me out.'

'There's always someone around,' I insist. Where the hell could Raybay be?

'Really, there's no one.'

Ok. I'm going to have to make a super human effort. I pull myself up, nod at Pat to follow me, and make my way carefully down the stairs. Each step is a challenge, my vision obscured by blotches. I'm constantly reminding myself who I am and what my mission is – to get Pat out of the front door and get myself back to my room where I can freak out in solitude. I'm covered in a horrible film of hot sweat. I don't know if I'm going to faint, shit my pants or throw up from one moment to the next. 'Are you ok?' I ask Pat again. 'You can sleep over if you want.'

'I'm fine,' she says again.

Finally I'm looking at her on the other side of the door. 'Sorry about this,' I say, and I close the door. Half of my mission is over.

I make my way back up the stairs and into what I think is my room, but something's wrong. The bed isn't where I expect it to be, but considering the state of me, it's hardly surprising that I can't remember where the bed is. I sense I'm not alone, but that doesn't matter, I just want to lie down. I hold onto someone. My leg still kicks from time to time. I see little ghosts in front of my eyes, like little space invaders, moving around the room. I feel warm hands on me.

*

I've been asleep. I wake up thanks to an awful retching at the back of my throat. I curse the fact that I share a bathroom and worry someone will see me and the state I'm in. I wonder how I can guarantee getting to the toilet without a load of people seeing me. I'm hesitating about what to do when I realise I'm not in my own bed.

I'm in an unfamiliar room sandwiched between two naked bodies. I try to wriggle out of the tangled mass of flesh and that's when I realise something's plugged in my arse. A large muscular arm is draped over me from behind, I can feel dry crusty matter all over me, which pinches my body hair. This must be one hell of a dream.

But dream or no dream, I have to get to the bathroom, and I make no effort to be slow or quiet as I wrench myself out from the hold. I'm up and standing, but then I have no idea where to go as I don't know whose room I'm in or where the nearest bathroom is, or even where my clothes are. Then my stomach heaves and I barf right where I'm standing. The puke hits the wooden floor with force and splatters far in every direction. With the cake out of my system I want to lie back down again. On the bed lies a completely naked Laura, the mousy teacher... and Belé. They're passed out. I want to pass out too, but I know that if I lie down, I won't be getting back up for some time.

I don't have the energy to look for my clothes and I walk stark naked into the corridor, up a flight of stairs, and then I realise my location in the house. I'd walked into Belé's room, which is directly below mine. No one is around to see me; lucky old me.

I get back to my room. It's surprisingly early in the evening; Anja hasn't even returned from band practice. I collapse onto the bed and in that moment feel very thankful. For the first time since I started feeling the effects of the space cake, I'm pretty confident I'm not going to die.

28th September 2005

I sense Anja come home in the middle of the night. I'm feeling rough in the morning and I tell her the amusing part of the night – about cooking a household's worth of potatoes and pasta, managing to get Pat out of the house, the hallucinations and the physical convulsions. I don't mention throwing up and doing god knows what else in Belé's room.

But the true horror of the knock on effect of the space cake is only beginning to unfold. Where do I begin?

It seems I've partaken in a three-way sandwich with Laura and Belé, and I was the filling; and I've cracked my ribs somewhere along the line. It hurts to breathe. It hurts to move. I picture myself teaching all my classes sitting down, not moving, and talking as little as possible. 'You probably fell without remembering,' Anja says. 'Do you want to go the doctor?'

I certainly don't. Ribs repair themselves, don't they?

Belé's dog ate some of the cake and it's in hospital. Will it survive? They're not sure.

And someone else ended up in hospital. Pat called with quite a story.

She left the Bowles thinking she was ok. She walked to Bülowstrasse and was on the U2 going back to Mitte when it hit her. She could hardly breathe, see or stand, but didn't think she'd be physically able to ask anyone for their seat. She checked what the next station was and called her brother. 'Jackson! It's Pat. I need you to pick me up at Potsdamer Platz!'

'What?' asked brother-Jackson.

'I'm in trouble! Come and get me!'

'Are you ok?'

She was too self-conscious to tell him what had happened in front of everyone on the train. 'Look, I just need you to come and get me!'

'What's the matter?'

She hung up.

Her brother was frantic with worry and rode his bicycle as fast as he could across the city. He didn't focus on the road and crashed into a parked car. He flew over the bonnet and fell on his knee. The pain eventually subsided enough that he managed to get back onto his bike and to Potsdamer Platz.

He found Pat. She told him everything and they walked slowly to her place. She had to sit down every few minutes to deal with the hallucinations. Her brother said, 'I'd be worried about you if I didn't know it was just a bit of cake.' They got to the Tacheles, and Pat's brother put her to bed.

Pat couldn't get up the following morning and missed the first day of her new job. The gallery said they weren't interested in someone who couldn't turn up to their first day and fired her.

As for Jackson, once he'd taken care of Pat, he realised the pain in his knee was excruciating and he took himself to hospital, and he's still there.

Then there's the really crazy thing that happened. The sad irony of this tragedy is that Raybay is teetotal and doesn't smoke weed or knowingly eat space cake. He saw the cake in the kitchen and no one was around to warn him about it because they were all off somewhere having a bad trip. He ate a slice with his coffee then went to his workshop to do some carpentry. Using an electric saw to cut through a piece of wood, he heard two thuds. He actually looked around for a moment wondering what the sound could have been. He turned off the saw and put it down, felt a sensation in his hand, and realised he'd sliced off two of his fingers. He called an ambulance and they got him to hospital just in time to reattach and save one, but not the other.

29th September 2005

Pat's brother's knee is badly damaged. It's in a cast and he has a long run of operations ahead. He was supposed to study in Australia this year and whether that will happen is in serious doubt.

Belé's dog isn't going to die, and Belé is celebrating by making... another space cake. Same recipe.

10th October 2005

The Bowles is celebrating its twenty-fifth anniversary, twenty-five years of squatters' rights, dirt-cheap rents, plenums, communal dinners that go into the night and end up in the club downstairs, slipper-wearing punks, the odd famous literary resident, halls full of bicycles... and great parties. They try to have one big blowout every year when they have enough money in the kitty, but they've been looking forward to this one especially. This is the big two-five.

We pull the garbage cans onto the street so we can use the garbage door as the party-entrance (invitees only, including some of the original housemates); we close the usual entrance and ship all the bikes out of the entrance hall so it can be a dance space; the Mecca Küche is a second dance space and has a huge food-spread; and bands are playing in different bedrooms and in the *Hof* (courtyard).

The Hof is the largest party area, containing two free bars, and two jumbo-fridges full of half-litre beers. Pictures are projected onto a wall of back-in-the-day, with builders, electricians and plumbers making the post-war shell of a building habitable. Fairy-lights hang from the roof down the full length of the Bowles, surrounding us in a magical cylinder of light under the starry night.

Since the space cake debacle, Belé ignores me. It's hard to say if his actions are any different than they were before. It's the same with Laura; she was never one for a friendly smile or prolonged eye-contact. I'm happy to sacrifice the clothes I lost that night if it means not ever having the incident mentioned. Well, I was partial to the blue jumper I'd been wearing, but many people lost a lot more than a jumper that evening.

Belé's on the decks, swaying side to side, with headphones round his neck and his hand in the air like a superstar DJ, his choice of techno resonating through the building. Anja's spending most of her time dancing in the hall, but I hate Belé too much to dance to any music he chooses to play.

I spend the early part of my evening talking to Matt and Momo. Matt is Laura's husband. He's stoically friendly to me, which is about as good as it gets in the Bowles. Matt and Laura have lived in the Bowles for a year, in my quarter, and a rift has started between this new generation of Bowles residents and old guard members like Momo.

Momo's lived in the Bowles almost since the beginning. He's also something of an ally of mine as he's a very old friend of Franka, Anja's mother. He doesn't know that one day I was shagging his wife so hard, I started bleeding all over his sofa.

Anyway, Matt and his quarter have started having dinner parties. Momo feels that an exclusive young-people's club has been created. Matt feels like this is an unfair accusation and that though the likes of Momo always hark on about 'community', all they're really concerned about is getting the best rooms, frowning upon anyone else having a good time and – hypocrisy of hypocrisies – Momo has a lock on his door! Doesn't this go against all that the Bowles stands for?

I strain to follow the argument through the techno, chatter, clinking bottles and laughter; and I'm not that interested. Why organise a huge party then spend the whole evening arguing about the Bowles? Their voices get louder as the conversation descends into an all-out shouting match and I slip away.

Into the Mecca Küche in search of pasta salad, I'm pleased by the friendly-yellow walls glowing in the party light. This is something I love about the Bowles, those bright colours, along with the quirky, odd-looking characters who spend their time arguing and dancing in strange outfits.

In my good mood, I sidle up to a woman with luscious long blonde hair, helping herself to a vol-au-vent. 'I made those,' I say in a low voice... to Anja's sister. 'Oh, hi there, Katja.'

'Hi there, funny man.' Katja smiles dryly.

'Nice to see you,' I say, trying to recover from flirtation-mode. 'Anja said you'd be here. Are your parents around?'

'Yes, they're right behind you.'

I swing around. 'Oh! It's my German family. How are you all?'

Franka smiles. 'We are well, Paul. We are disappointed we don't see more of you.'

'I'd have thought you've seen too much of me.'

They stare at me.

'Because we were all naked in the sauna together,' I explain.

'When you had a big erection,' Wolfgang says.

'Yes,' I say. The humour has dissipated from the conversation.

'We just can't work you out, Paul,' Franka says.

'I'm an enigma,' I say, trying to be charismatic.

'Enigma,' Katja repeats. 'Did you think I wouldn't get that reference? The machine used for deciphering Nazi messages during the war.'

'Is it?'

'You can't help it, can you? You've got prejudice running through your veins...'

Her face is red with fury. She looks like she's about to throw a drink in my face. What's there to say?

I turn and bolt.

Wolfgang calls after me, 'Paul! We need to talk about your insurance bills. You owe a lot of money!'

I head to the nearest bar and knock back a shot of vodka, then a shot of something else. Then another. Then I feel better. I grab a fresh beer, and find Raybay on an empty terrace looking down on the party, sitting on a chair with a bottle of his non-alcoholic beer in his three-finger hand. We look at the happy faces.

My mind wanders to a book Pat showed me recently called *Place of Memories, Jewish daily life in Berlin neighbourhoods*. It was strange to see pictures of my *Kiez* (neighbourhood) back in the day, and of course there were heart-wrenching stories of the lives that were cut short by the Nazis, and at the back it listed the names of citizens taken away from their homes and deported to concentration camps. I scrolled down the list and sure enough found the Bowles. There were five people taken out of the building and sent to Theresienstadt; they all died within months.

The following evening I was sitting in the plenum as the Bowles-people argued for hours about the Matt-Momo thing.

'You are only being sociable with part of the Bowles community.'

'But you put locks on your doors, what's 'community' about that?'

It's insane.

For all the talking that happens in the Bowles, I find it fitting that Pat showed me the most interesting fact I knew about the place.

Now I'm thinking about Pat, and it hurts.

As if he can read my mind, Raybay asks me, 'Where's your friend tonight?'

'Pat? She's out of town, a kickboxing tournament.'

'It must be hard being friends with someone you'd like to fuck,' he says smiling.

I crack up. I love this guy.

'Yeah, it's hard.'

'Maybe you could be more than friends. But you're with Anja.'

'I know. I don't know what I'm doing.'

'You choose not to be with the one you love because you have a very low opinion of yourself.'

I laugh again. For a man who doesn't seem to be interested in anything, he's watchful. He might just have hit the nail on the head too.

Then Raybay tells me a story. Actually he tells it to me three times and I have to ask him twenty questions before I understand it, but it goes like this:

When he was a young man in who-knows-what-decade, he was riding a night train from Budapest to Krakow. It's a notorious train; where local knaves are known to release sleeping gas in your cabin then rob you. He got on the train and found an empty seat in a cabin with one other person, a young woman; she was dressed smartly and had long, angelic, almost-white hair. He ignored her like he expected she wanted him to but she seemed intrigued by him and started a conversation. It turned out she loved punk. She didn't look like a punk, Raybay said, and she rolled her eyes and said that she chose not to dress up like one but outside of her job, all she did was listen to punk and go to gigs. They liked all the same music and talked about the scene and hours flew by.

Then a group of overweight men with moustaches stood outside the glass door of their cabin, watching them. 'Maybe they want to join us,' the girl said. She was lying down on her side of the cabin and said they should pretend to be asleep so they wouldn't be disturbed.

On the contrary, Raybay said, and he told her why the train was so notorious. So they kept each other awake throughout the whole night by telling each other stories, and they were right to. In the morning they discovered that people in nearly all the other cabins had had their clothes and bags ripped apart with knives and all their money stolen.

Raybay and the girl swapped addresses and he waited with her until her friend came to pick her up. He was in disbelief that he'd met a girl like that... then he was in disbelief that later that very day, his bag was stolen and he lost her address. He also couldn't believe that the woman actually wrote to him for years, and it was so frustrating because she never wrote down her return address. Eventually she said that she knew he wasn't going to reply and she didn't even know if he was receiving the letters so she wouldn't write anymore.

He never forgot her, and years later at a UK Subs gig he saw a familiar face. He walked up to a woman and asked if they had met before. The woman looked at him and said that he was familiar too but she didn't know where from. They parted and only later did he realise that she was the friend who'd picked up the girl from the train station.

'I always go to UK Subs gigs wondering if I will see them again,' he says.

'But it was years ago. Would you even recognise her?' I ask.

'I don't know,' Raybay says. 'But I always wonder. She could have been the one.'

'That's a really sad story. Sorry, man.'

'If something happens and you think it's fate,' he said, 'It's a pity to waste it.'

'You mean Pat? But the reason I like her is that she's a free spirit. She's had boyfriends, but then she leaves them.'

'It might be different with you.'

I light a cigarette and ruminate. To be with Pat. It would be unimaginable, too good to stand. Imagine the disappointment of raising my hopes up and finding out it would never be. Best not to think about it.

Belé makes a charismatic announcement that the entertainment is about to begin and plays a jazz tune – a welcome change to the music that's been banging away all evening.

Jade is a good friend of Anja's. She's small and round with long dark frizzy hair. She smiles hello to me and I to her, but frustratingly we can't communicate more than that. She doesn't speak a word of English and when I attempt to talk to her in my bad German I don't get anywhere.

She's going to do her flame twirling act.

The east side of the Hof is elevated and makes a good stage. She lights her balls, so to speak, and starts swinging the balls of flame round herself, carving graceful shapes into the night in time with the music, becoming a blur of light and heat.

I watch, impressed; finish my beer, and am frustrated to see that the two beer fridges are located behind Jade. Then I see that people in the same predicament simply walk onto the stage and around her to casually get themselves a beer. Jade loses her rhythm and stumbles, but manages to pick up her momentum again.

'Jesus!' I yell. 'What do they think they're doing? She's fire dancing and they walk past her to get a beer?'

'They are stupid,' Raybay says in his world-weary tone.

'You know,' I say in amazed anger, 'There is something that is typically 'Berlin' about this. No one gives a fuck about anyone else.'

'That's the appeal,' Raybay says. 'People move here from small towns where everyone knows them. Here they are anonymous because no one gives a fuck.'

People keep passing her to get drinks, and the dance becomes so tense, I'm urging her not to slip and set herself on fire. When she finally has enough space to check around herself, she slows down the momentum of the balls, douses the flames and leaves the stage before the first song has ended. There is muted applause, and I can see she doesn't look too happy as she walks away from the stage and sits down by herself.

I wait and no one goes to her, so I go to check if she's ok. There are tears in her eyes and she's holding a cold beer on a bad burn on her thigh. 'Oh shit! Are you ok? Um... *bist du ok?*'

'*Nein!*' she says, crying.

'We need an ambulance... um...' All my German has escaped me. I say to her very slowly, 'Hos-pi-tal?'

She shakes her head at me blankly.

'Doctor?'

'*Ja! Doktor.*'

I manage to communicate with hand gestures that she should sit still while I take care of things. I find Anja and tell her what's happened. 'She's badly burned. She needs to go to hospital.'

'Oh no,' Anja says, without her party smile completely leaving her lips. 'You should get someone to call for an ambulance.'

That's what I'm doing. I say, 'Yes, I don't have a phone. I lost it on space cake night.'

'Oh, mine is upstairs.'

'Well... I could go and get it?' I suggest.

'Sure,' Anja says without much concern. Her body is still moving to the music.

Does it not commute when something bad has happened? Is life through her eyes so much like an episode of *Sesame Street*?

I try to hurry but the milling crowd make it difficult. I get Anja's phone and take it straight to Jade. She says German things into the phone. I confirm with her, '*Doktor?*'

'*Doktor,*' she nods, wincing in pain. I wrap up some ice in a tea towel for her to hold on the burn, and she gets up to go outside to wait for the ambulance. I put my arm around her and lead her out, and I look around in disbelief at everyone ignoring us. Anja is spinning on the dance floor with an arm extended to the sky.

We wait in the street and the car arrives. Two men help her in. One speaks English and asks me, 'Are you her friend?'

I say, 'Yes,' and get in the car with her.

We wait for thirty minutes at the hospital for a doctor. Jade has her eyes closed, focused on bearing the pain. Tears roll down her cheeks. Finally she's given a bed and some painkillers, and the doctor tells me she should stay overnight.

Eventually, I'm told I have to leave. Jade says, 'Danke,' with tender eyes and squeezes my hand.

I get off the train at Bülowstrasse and walk back to the Bowles. Purificacion is outside smoking. She looks like a femme fatale from an old noir picture, wonderfully curvaceous, with long dark silky hair, gazing at me like Barbara Stanwyck looks at that guy in *Double Indemnity*. She's wearing a small, brown leather jacket, and jeans that look like they'd been painted on. I watch her cigarette move towards her red lips hungrily.

'Where have you been, Paul?' she asks.

I tell her what's happened

She seems genuinely concerned. She puts her hand on her heart and says something comforting in Spanish.

'Let's go to your room,' I say.

She looks surprised for a moment, then says, 'We can take the first staircase to miss the party.'

She walks ahead of me, and I'm right behind her when she opens the door to her apartment. We can hear the techno-beats and muffled party sounds from outside. She's usually safe in the knowledge that her husband isn't home and I like the compromising position I've put her in.

I push her against a wall and undress her completely. She tries to do the same to me but I hold her wrists. She wriggles out of my grasp and moves to the sofa, crawling over it in slow motion, creating an inviting sexual pose. She yelps as I grab her by the ankles and pull her back towards me.

I slam into her hard and enjoy seeing her efforts not to scream, biting onto anything she can get her mouth round.

She laughs with surprise when I pull off my rubber and shoot everything all over her, and she puts her hand on my chest when I collapse onto the floor next to her.

I hardly notice that she's gone into the bathroom. I stand up but have to sit back down. I'm surprised at how dizzy I am, and after I catch my breath, I go to open a window and look down at the party from a discreet angle. The fresh air feels good. Hot from doing the deed fully clothed, I take off my shirt and dry my upper body with a tea-towel.

La gorda, Purificacion's fat cat approaches me. I'm generally liked by cats and dogs. I usually hold out my hand and they approach and allow themselves to be stroked. La gorda doesn't feel that way about me. The only time I tried to stroke it, it clawed me deep on my finger, and since then it's ignored me. It doesn't seem particularly friendly to anyone. I find it strange how Purificacion pours so much love and attention into an animal that's so unaffectionate. She's always picking it up, hugging it, playing with it and kissing it on the belly.

So I find it strange that La gorda is approaching me now. I feel the scratch it gave me last time and wonder if I should be worried. Suddenly it leaps upwards and I have no time to position myself to catch it. Then I realise, it's not leaping towards me, but out of the open window.

I make a lame attempt to grab it and scream, 'Stupid fucking cat!'

I see it fly into the night, then downwards into the Hof. Spreading itself like it expects that will help. I don't hear the sound of it crashing over the sound of everyone's screams.

There's a crowd around where it lands. Then they look up at me, shirtless, leaning out of Purificacion's window like the idiot I am.

I can read it on everyone's face: *Who's that? Paul? What's he doing up there? Oh, of course.*

I search for Anja's face and find it. Eyes wide, her hands over her mouth, horror pose.

30th November 2005

Haven't written in a while.

Feel too sick.

The heartache.

It's over with Anja.

And the Bowles.

Pat's doing everything she can to help me stay in Berlin. I stayed with her in her small studio at the top of the Tacheles, a haze of party sounds and the waft of ganja all day and night.

Just as she had gone through listings to find me teaching work, she found me an amazingly cheap place to live, and borrowed a car to help me move my things.

My new home is on the historical Sophienstrasse in Mitte. Part of the ironically intact Jewish quarter. It was settled in the end of the seventeenth century. Small brass tiles with a name, birthdate, name of a concentration camp, and a death date, are scattered around the pavement in memory of the lives, families and friendships that existed here before they were destroyed. The nineteenth-century houses were restored during the GDR as a tourist attraction, giving the place a slightly kitsch, TV-set quality.

What's typical of a GDR tourist attraction is that only the façades are attractive. Once you walk through the first house of the apartment building, then the second (which is officially unsafe for *any* habitation) you come to the third, my dingy low-ceilinged home. I've been told not to make myself too comfortable, as the reason ordinary people like me can live in such a nice area is because it's the last dingy building left, that will soon be knocked down to make space for nicer, more expensive apartments.

Opposite is the Baroque Sophienkirche, the only church in Mitte to survive World War II, whose bells ring on the hour throughout the day... and night! The ringing wakes me up constantly and every time I wake I can't help but laugh at the comedy of it.

We have coal heating which never really warms the apartment up. You wake up cold, shovel coal into the oven and light it up. It takes three hours to take effect, at which point, we're out at work. It's cold by the time we get home, but we're so cold, we go through the same process, then it's too hot to sleep.

My flatmate is Nathan, a tall handsome American, who sleeps with a different, gorgeous woman practically every night. They start in the kitchen, where he cooks pasta. Maybe I'll be there to help things along with a bit of conversation. Then Nathan offers to play his guitar and he and his latest conquest disappear into his room. He plays *The Drugs Don't Work*, then I hear humping.

It's hardly the most romantic number to seduce a *Fräulein* with. 'Do you know any other songs?' I ask him.

He doesn't.

He studies film and one afternoon he takes me to nearby Auguststrasse, which contains a lot of galleries and art-space, to preview a film his classmate has made about her divorce. It's a well put together slice of her life, recording her thoughts and how she looked in a time that'll never return as she and her husband divide their things and deal with all the bureaucracy involved. It ends amusingly, the credits say A FILM BY... and it shows her hyphened, married name, then letters are deleted until only her maiden name is left.

15th December 2005

Nathan is old-school, like me. I mean to say, he likes old, crusty things, not the new and shiny. And he introduces me to Café Cinema, the oldest surviving café in the spanking new tourist area of Hackesher Markt. The walls are adorned with beautifully taken black and white shots of ordinary people drinking in the café. 'Ordinary people made to look like film stars,' Nathan says. The darkness and sparse candlelight gives the place an unreal quality. 'Living in Mitte is like being in a movie,' is a typical thing that the endearingly flamboyant Nathan will say. 'That's why it's important to look good. If you think about your life as a film, you want to look the part.'

It becomes mine and Pat's new local as we now share the same neighbourhood. She likes hearing about Nathan's exploits. 'German girls love guitar players,' she explains. I wonder if she'd be able to resist his charm.

'Maybe I should stand under Anja's window and serenade her.'

Pat rolls her eyes. 'Now Anja doesn't want to see you, you are hopelessly in love with her.'

'I always loved her! I moved countries for her! Does that mean nothing?'

'Do you think you'll leave Berlin now?'

'I miss her so much. Everything here reminds me of her. Yes, maybe I'll go back to London.'

'Is she the problem? You didn't seem to like her very much when you were with her.'

'What would you know?!'

'It doesn't matter where you try to escape to, Paul. You can't escape yourself.'

I blow a raspberry.

'Have you tried speaking to her?'

'I've called, texted, emailed, I've even spoken to her mother. *She* had a theory. She said Anja had had an unhealthy infatuation with me. All men fawn over her so she found it appealing that I ignored her and didn't seem to like her very much. She saw me as a challenge.'

'Do you think she's right?'

'I don't know!' I say, welling up. 'I just miss her. I *miss* her!'

'Boy, I really don't understand men.'

'No one said you did.'

'At least I know not to open someone's upstairs window if they have a cat.'

'How could I have known that?'

'What happened to it anyway?

'It survived.'

'Really?'

'Yes, it just broke its legs.'

'Ouch.'

'That reminds me, is your brother still going to study in Australia?'

'That's not going to happen now. His injury is pretty serious. He's developed rheumatism.'

'Oh nuts.'

'What about the Mexican lady and her husband?'

'They're breaking up and both moving out of the Bowles.'

'Jesus.'

'I know. They had the best room too.'

'You seem to bring bad luck to people.'

'*She's* actually leaving *him*. She didn't seem to like him. Now she's got a visa...'

'You don't really have any moral high ground here, Paul.'

'Thanks.'

My mind drifts as I outwardly carry on conversing with Pat. Then she catches my attention by mentioning what had happened between *us* at the Kitkatclub for the first time since it had happened.

'...between us in the club...' I was sure she said.

'It did,' I agree, keeping my expression blank until I can catch onto what she's talking about.

Pat says, 'Now that you're single, I wondered, maybe sometime in the future, maybe we could be together.'

And I recall, yes, I had had feelings for Pat, but now I can't get Anja out of my head.

'I don't know. It's too soon,' I say.

Pat shrugs like it's no big deal.

We hang out a lot like we've always done. But it never feels like a good time, just a distraction. I always have this dreadful sinking feeling inside. Without Anja, there's just nothing else. I grieve the loss of how she used to look at me and encourage my writing.

So I write.

And realise I'm an atrocious writer. The problem with a story is the same problem as with the Bowles, it has other people in it. How do people act? What do people say? I read over my journal in the hope it will help me, imagining it'll sound like Isherwood.

It's horrible, and in this smarmy voice that even I hate. Where Isherwood was a real observer, my characters weren't well-drawn. They weren't even amusingly scribbled. I just didn't listen to or know any of these people I'd spent the past months with. They were just a background in a scene where Paul, the main idiot, appears and performs his latest screw up.

Anja... who was this person I'd lived with for all that time?

As I start to question whether I know anyone at all, Pat is talking to me and I study her features, and she becomes unfamiliar. Am I capable of actually knowing anyone? When I look back on all the things this Paul-guy did to the woman he sincerely loved, I don't know that guy. I didn't even know myself. If Anja hadn't kicked me out, would I still be there, treating her like a bastard?

And I do see the irony that I'm thinking all this while Pat is talking to me, thinking I'm listening to her.

10th October 2006

After the shock of seeing the drivel I've written and my realisation that I don't care about or really know anyone including myself, I'm determined to be less wretched and to make a better effort with others. I mean, all we are is the connections we make with other people. Once I start consciously listening, I enjoy writing more and start to get somewhere with the story I've been working on.

I get into a routine of teaching and writing, and drinking in Café Cinema with Pat. The winter is more traumatising than I could have imagined. I didn't know Berlin got so much colder that London. My pathetic English winter coat simply won't do and I discover the need to wear long johns. You only go outside for necessity and when you do, the parts of your body left exposed (obviously your eyes and nose so you can see and breathe) are painful for hours afterwards.

It's like a different place because Berlin is an outdoor city. There are so many parks and cafés with outdoor spaces. And the cold season lasts so long. In February when I dare to imagine the worst of it is over, it's hardly begun.

But summer finally returns and once again we can ride our bikes and though it's warm, many women will only wear skirts or shorts with thick leggings underneath, still traumatised by the cold, dark winter.

The one year anniversary of the day I arrived in Berlin came, and I went out drinking with Pat to distract myself from my overactive nostalgia, so now she insists we celebrate the day I left the Bowles.

We start our session off in a pizza place in Mitte. We have a few bottles of Sternburg and Pat's telling me a story about how her uncle has just died. She's inherited something, but won't go to court to claim it. When I ask her why not, she says that when you inherit something in Germany, you're not told what it is, and it could very well be debt. So the safest thing to do is say you don't want it. If you accept it and it turns out to be debt, there's no going back. Madness! But quite amusing madness.

Autumn suits her so well, the warm comfortable way she dresses and her hair has natural streaks of red and light brown. She's telling her story the way she tells stories, laughing her head off, so alive and so vibrant with that fantastic large grin of hers. It's one of those luminous Berlin autumn days. I don't know what music is playing, but it's a beautiful violin piece, Bach or something. I'm looking at Pat and I cannot believe how lucky I am that I'm sitting here with her. It feels like fate, getting a drink in Ostzone the same time that Anja did, and all I learned from our relationship and break-up, and the way that this moment has arrived, with this person I bumped into at one of Anja's gigs, then she *happened* to work in a café two minutes from where I lived – this woman I knew I would never forget, even after just two minutes of banal conversation and thinking I'd never see her again.

I want to complete the moment, to lean over and kiss her, but she's sitting too far away. I'd have to stand up, step over a low table, my legs would be astride hers, then I wouldn't be able to bend down to kiss her, I'd be too close to her, and she'd be wondering what the hell I'm doing...

So I don't know what I'm going to do when *she* does something. Without looking me in the eye, she says, 'Paul, the day before we met – without really consciously doing it – I was sitting by the Spree and I threw a coin into the river and made a wish...' She shakes her head with embarrassment for what she's saying. 'I hadn't met anyone in a long time who'd made me feel anything. When I met you...' she pushes the words out from her stomach, '... I felt something. I still do.'

For the woman of your dreams to be saying this to you – just as you have been thinking pretty much the same thing – is like a ridiculous dream. But what else is there to do but accept it like it's actually happening?

We're holding hands across the table and so begins the happiest time of my life.

5th January 2007

The happiest time of my life, the autumn colours, the walks in the park, the winter approaching and Pat spending all her time in my flat because my coal heating is actually better than hers, and having dinner every night with Nathan and his newest ladyfriend going through their methodical motions, and lazy days in bed cuddling, watching films and the sex and her translucent skin and her smiling eyes... I don't worry about whether I'm good enough for her or if I'm making her happy, I'm just happy.

And then it ends. It really spoils the poetic end of my story: naïve London boy comes to Berlin, makes a lot of mistakes, learns a lot, changes his ways, stops resisting and embraces the culture, falls into a blissful relationship which – it seems – the universe has created, then three months later, Pat says she prefers being single. Sure she 'loves' me and says she doesn't think she'll meet anyone else she'd rather spend her life with.

'I just don't want to be in a relationship,' she says. 'Things are just more fun on your own, you know?'

And this is heart-breaking, and it strikes me as very 'Berlin'. I hear it's the city with the largest proportion of single people. In Europe? In the world? I'm not sure. I'm not even sure how they created that statistic but I believe it. The rest of the world, I feel, is a place for couples. In England, when I say I'm single people nod and smile at me looking like they're wondering if something's wrong with me or if I just haven't met the right person yet. In Berlin, if you say you're in a relationship people nod and smile as if to say, 'I'm sorry, is being young and cool, and going out and having fun every night, making the most of life and being an independent man, too much for you?'

Thanks

I wrote this story some years ago and stuck it in a drawer. Thanks to Matt Potter who encouraged and helped put it into print. He's to blame for all this really.

About the Author

Jason S. Andrews is a writer and London tour guide.

His work has appeared in *Bordercrossing Berlin*, *Pure Slush*, *Sand Journal* and *Skyscanner*.

For more about the author, visit his website at www.jasonsandrews.com.

Other books from
Truth Serum Press

Luck and Other Truths
by Richard Mark Glover
ISBN: 978-1-925101-77-5

From the misadventures of a Dade County cop going through burnout in the Spanish Main to a doubting soldier in the battlements of Iraq, "Lieutenant, you're a dumb mother-fucker," these stories wrench the reader and make him think. Richard Mark Glover's stories resemble the man himself, free, wide-ranging, erudite and willing to dangle over barrancas like an alpine mountaineer.

What Came Before
by Gay Degani
ISBN: 978-1-925536-05-8

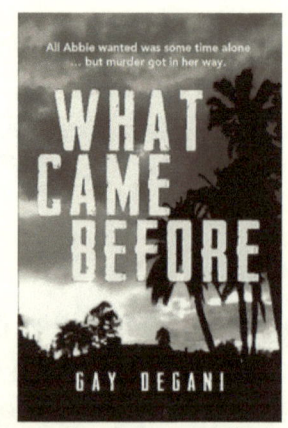

Five words scribbled on a discarded piece of paper ignite old memories for Abbie Palmer and leads to the explosive uncovering of a fifty-year-old mystery. *What Came Before*, Gay Degani's debut novel rumbles along at breakneck speed. I've long enjoyed the quirky characters and tightly-written plots of Ms. Degani's short stories and her novel didn't disappoint me.

happyme@t.us
by Kim Conklin
ISBN: 978-1-925536-07-2

To be everywhere and nowhere, all at once ... Through her stories, Kim Conklin takes us on a journey of the human condition, where the everyday becomes foreign and dangerous, while the oddities of our world provide us with strange comfort. Each story is unsettling, passionate, thoughtful, provocative and reaffirming; taking the reader everywhere and nowhere, all at once. Dark tales, deftly told.

Rain Check
by Levi Andrew Noe
ISBN: 978-1-925536-09-6

Beautifully rendered, the stories in *Rain Check* could well be the footprints and photographs of our own lives if we'd have taken risks as daring as Noe's characters. Reading these stories is like being a lucky voyeur who happens upon an artist with brush in hand, nearing the finishing touch of their masterpiece. Nothing is more potent than prose that lifts off the page and lands, like a well-placed bullet or caress, on the heart, and that's precisely what Noe has done here.

La Ronde

by Townsend Walker

ISBN: 978-1-925101-64-5

La Ronde sweeps you up into a beguiling tale of greed, mistaken identity, and desire. A chilling novella with characters that pop off the page and events that make you squirm, it makes you wonder: what would your spouse do if he or she wanted to kill you?

Based on True Stories

by Matt Potter

ISBN: 978-1-925101-75-1

These gems provoke, like the tip of a chef's knife pricking skin, and just as the words get uncomfortable, the story delivers the bit of redemption that reveals the humanity of his characters – and of us all. These stories are real, raw, and honest.

The Miracle of Small Things

by Guilie Castillo Oriard

ISBN: 978-1-925101-73-7

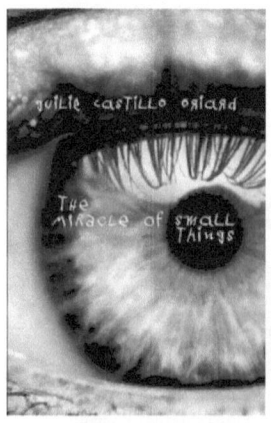

Told deftly, with humor and insight into our very human vulnerabilities, this lovely novella builds upon that quest for happiness we share, a sense of belonging, and makes me want to travel south to find my own miracle.

www.ingramcontent.com/pod-product-compliance
Lightning Source LLC
Chambersburg PA
CBHW031607260626
47154CB00020B/1698